IN TOO DEEP

LOVE UNDERCOVER, BOOK 1

LK SHAW

For Kerri
Your strength and bravery was a testament to what an incredible woman you were. No matter what odds were against you, you never gave up. I miss you, friend.

Kerri Lynn James
1974 – 2018

Want a **FREE** short story?
What about **FREE** chapters of **FOREVER** delivered to your inbox?

Be sure to sign up for my newsletter and download your copy of A Birthday Spanking, a Doms of Club Eden prequel! You'll also start receiving bi-weekly chapters of the novella Forever

You'll also receive infrequent updates about what I'm working on, alerts for sales and new releases, and other stuff I don't share elsewhere!

Doms of Club Eden
Submission

Desire

Redemption

Protect

Betrayal

My Christmas Dom

Absolution

Forever (A prequel) - Coming July 2020

Love Undercover Series
In Too Deep

Striking Distance

Atonement

Other Books
Love Notes: A Dark Romance

SEALs in Love

Say Yes

Black Light: Possession

Saving Evie: A Brotherhood Protectors

PROLOGUE

"Kill him."

Those two, single-syllable words played on repeat like a litany in my ears. They were accompanied by a multitude of emotions.

Horror.

Guilt.

Satisfaction.

It's the last one that made me the most nervous.

I tried to pinpoint the exact moment things changed. The moment *I* changed. Was it the first time I took a hit of blow and loved the rush it provided? The time I sat on a piss-scented couch with a gun in my face, its hammer drawn back as incentive, while I "sampled" the latest stash of a new-to-me dealer who didn't quite trust me? Or maybe it was when I realized that sometimes, in order to make things happen, you had to get your hands dirty. I was on my own. No cavalry was coming to my rescue. I did what I had to to survive, even if I hated myself most of the time.

The drugs.

The killing.

They were all a part of the man I'd become over the last five years in order to bring an entire organization crumbling to the ground. It was my life's mission. My obsession, in fact.

Like an out of body experience, I watched my hand remove the gun from its shoulder holster and point it at the bleeding man begging for his life on his knees in front of me.

"Please, don't do this. I told you where the money was. Please, I have a wife, a daught—"

Closing off my emotions, I squeezed the trigger. The bullet entered his brain, cutting his words off mid-sentence. The dead man collapsed onto the cement floor of the abandoned warehouse near Chicago's Lake Michigan, blood pooling next to his head.

Miguel Álvarez, the man who'd given the death order, spat in the direction of the body. "Let that be another lesson to those who steal from me."

He clapped me on the shoulder on his way to the black sedan parked just inside the warehouse doors. "Tomás, my friend, welcome to the family."

I remained there, unmoving, while I watched two men begin to wrap up the body for disposal. It would be weighed down and dumped in the waters of the Michigan, hopefully to never be found again. My expression remained impassive.

"You will come to the house, *sí*?" The voice called from behind my back. Forcing my eyes from the scene in front of me, I turned to face Miguel.

"Yes, sir, I'll be there soon. I have some quick business to take care of first." I didn't flinch at his assessing stare. After a moment he nodded.

"Don't be long, Tomás." The warning tone was clear. "I want to introduce you to my nephew, Alejandro."

He disappeared inside the car, closing the door behind him. The Mercedes pulled away, and I continued to watch it until the tail lights disappeared. Leaving the cleanup crew to their task, I exited the stifling heat of the warehouse before jumping on my fully restored 1984 cherry red Harley Softail. I started her up, slammed my heel against the kickstand, and took off in the opposite direction Miguel had gone. Fifteen minutes later, I entered the Grant Park North parking garage and drove around until I reached the fourth level. I spotted an empty parking space next to a blue Honda. The passenger window of the Honda lowered at the same time I cut the engine.

"I'm in." I spoke to the shadowy figure of my handler sitting in the driver's seat without turning my head in her direction.

"What did you do?"

I gave a self-deprecating laugh. "What I had to, Landon."

There was a long pause. She finally replied with a voice full of understanding. "I see. Well, we both knew going in that something like this might happen. It's unfortunate, but it needed to be done. You'll be in touch soon, then?"

"Yes. I'll let you know when the next deal is going down."

Without another word, I cranked up the bike and took off. I drove down Michigan Avenue, burying my emotions. I'd been with the Drug Enforcement Administration for eight years. I was en route to the home of the man in charge of the second largest Mexican cartel in the United States.

No longer was I Brody Thomas, D.E.A. agent. I was Tomás González, full-fledged member of the Juárez Cartel.

I ignored the guilt stabbing me deep in my gut. Diego Garcia may have been the first man I'd been forced to kill, but if I was going to bring down the cartel, he most likely wouldn't be my last. Besides, any man who got his wife hooked on dope and then prostituted her out to his friends earned a special place in hell.

There were so many different scenarios in which all this would be over. Oftentimes, in my dreams, I eradicated every drug off the street and was hailed a hero. Other times, I had occasional nightmares of my cover being blown and Álvarez having me killed. It didn't matter. I'd signed up knowing the risks. But never, at any time, did I envision it would be a sexy Latina bombshell who would eventually bring my world crashing down around me.

CHAPTER 1

"I'M SO NOT okay with this."

Victor spoke under his breath, keeping his gaze averted from my scantily clad body. I wore a fuchsia silk robe barely long enough to cover my ass cheeks. It kept draping open to reveal the black and pink lace bra which barely hid the shadowy darkness of my nipples.

"Not nearly as much as me," I countered, once again tugging and rearranging the damn robe to keep shit covered. I was extremely uncomfortable with my brother being here as my backup, but he'd told my Captain he didn't trust anyone else to keep me safe. It didn't matter that we didn't work the same precinct, Victor refused to let anyone else watch my back.

"I don't mean your outfit. I mean, I'm not okay with that either, but *this* in general." He made a sweeping gesture with his finger. "You being here. Someone else could have been sent in."

I stepped closer to Victor and looked around to make sure no one could hear our conversation. "This is for our brother, Victor. Do you really trust anyone else in the department to be as vigilant in searching for him as we'll be? The department is understaffed and overworked, even to look for one of their own."

He sighed. "I know, but I don't like this, Ines. We're talking about the cartel. What happens if you do catch the eye of Álvarez's nephew? There may be certain…expectations of you."

I sent him a look that said he was an idiot. "I'll deal with things as they come along. We both know they'll kill Ernesto if they find out he's a cop. I can't let that happen."

My father and brothers all worried about me joining the force five years ago, but I couldn't imagine being anything other than a police officer. Normally, none of the boys made too much of a fuss over an assignment handed to me. However, today was going to be one of those overprotective days.

I could understand their fear. Our eldest brother had been investigating a murder connected to Miguel Álvarez and the cartel when he'd gone missing. I'd had to convince my Lieutenant to let me go undercover at *Sweet SINoritas*, the strip club owned by Álvarez. A club his nephew was known to frequent. He was my way into the cartel, a way for me to search for Ernesto.

I'd made it abundantly clear that Victor wasn't to step foot on the main floor while I was working. It was bad enough having him in the dressing room. There was no way he was going to catch me flashing my tits and ass. I was also trying to keep those men alive, because there was a good chance my brother would kill someone if they saw them looking at me the wrong way.

My brother instinctively reached for his gun when the door to the dressing room suddenly swung open.

"Gabriela, you're up in five!" Mikey, the manager, hollered into the room before shutting the door again.

"That's my cue," I told Victor as I stood from the stool I'd been perched on. "Keep an eye on the other girls while I'm gone, will ya?"

"You know I will *Gabriela*, but you watch yourself out there. I don't like that I can't be out there to have your back." His tone was both worried and disgruntled.

"It's showtime."

Victor almost full-body shuddered in disgust as I fluffed my hair and pushed up my boobs before strolling out of the room and toward the stage, where the sound of my intro by the DJ grew louder.

THE FINAL NOTES OF PRINCE'S *GET OFF* FADED AS I GAVE ONE last bump and grind for the benefit of my target, who sat in the front row. He looked younger than I expected. Maybe because of the way he was dressed. He was the twenty-four year old son of Miguel Álvarez's only sister. After her death, when Alejandro was ten, he was sent to live with Miguel, who raised him. It was said he was being groomed to one day run the family business.

So I expected him to be wearing, at the least, business casual. Instead, he wore a white wife-beater accented with a ridiculous amount of gold chains. On one hand, he wore a gold pinky ring. I had no idea what his hair looked like, because his head was covered with a baseball cap. He also wore aviators. Inside. It's always sunny in Doucheville.

It had taken me almost half the song to get his attention, but once I had it, he was hooked. He'd removed his sunglasses and his eyes never left me while I danced. Now that my set was over, I gathered up the bills scattered on the stage before exiting down the stairs at the back of the stage where Mikey stood waiting. I handed off the loose bills, and he added them to my cashbox. At the end of the night all my money would be added together and the house would take their cut. Whatever was leftover was mine. On a typical night, I brought home almost three hundred. On a good night, I left with at least five.

I made my way to the bar so I could start serving drinks until my next set. I looked over my shoulder to see if I still had Alejandro's attention, and smiled to myself that I did. It seemed almost too easy. When I reached the bar, I grabbed a small serving tray and headed to my assigned tables. Every trip back and forth, I made sure to stroll past his table, sending the occasional shy, but not too-inviting smile his way. I'd just delivered a bottle of beer to one of the regulars when Mikey pulled me aside.

"It must be your lucky night, babe. Mr. Álvarez's nephew, Alejandro, wants to meet you." I could practically see the dollar signs in Mikey's eyes as he tried to inconspicuously point him out. I had no intention of telling him I already knew.

Playing it dumb, I asked, "Who's Mr. Álvarez?"

Mikey looked over his shoulder before leaning closer and lowering his voice. "Miguel Álvarez owns this club. It's a not-so-well-known fact that he's cartel."

I gave him my best shocked expression. "You're telling me this place is owned by the cartel?"

"Keep your voice down, for fuck's sake. We don't need the cops or the feds knocking on our door. This is a legitimate establishment."

I barely refrained from rolling my eyes. Everyone on the force knew what type of establishment this was, and legit certainly wasn't it. Sure, they paid their taxes, but there were so many illegal things going down in this place, it wasn't funny. My brother Pablo worked this precinct.

Mikey filled in the silence. "So, you better make sure you're extra nice to him."

Hands on my hips, I snapped, "I'm not a prostitute."

He held his hands up in a defensive gesture. "I'm not telling you to sleep with the kid. I'm merely telling you to be…nice."

With those words he turned and left me to interpret them.

I felt eyes on me, and when I looked around, Alejandro smiled and winked at me. I smiled, but quickly averted my eyes. This had been my goal the whole night. Make contact.

"Hi there," I greeted them timidly when I reached their table. "I'm Gabriela."

"What a beautiful name for a beautiful woman."

I giggled vapidly. "Thank you. You must be Alejandro."

"*Sí*," he replied while he eye-fucked me. "Why don't you join us? Have a drink."

Knowing Mikey expected me to be "nice", I accepted. I spent the rest of the night mildly flirting and being overly impressed with Alejandro and all his flash. I wasn't sure if I should have been offended or not, but it barely took any effort on my part before he was inviting me back to his place. Thankfully, the Rohypnol I slipped in his beer took effect before he could do more than plaster me with a few sloppy kisses and cop a quick feel. After he'd passed out, I tugged off his pants and threw a blanket on top of him. It was going to be a long night.

I'd told myself when I'd come up with this plan that I would do whatever it took to find Ernesto, even sleep with the enemy. But in the end, I couldn't. I kept thinking "what if?" *What if I never found my brother? What if I wound up pregnant? What if, in the end, it would destroy me?*

When Alejandro woke the next morning, I was already up and making breakfast, making him think we'd had a great time. Especially since I'd chucked my clothes on his bedroom floor and was walking around the kitchen wearing one of his shirts. Anything to give credence to the idea we slept together. I soon became a permanent fixture on his arm. Everything was going as planned, until I met *him*.

CHAPTER 2

WHOOSH. That was the sound of cocaine rushing up my nostril as I snorted the line. My eyes watered and immediately, I could feel the high take effect. The urge to try a little more was powerful, but I squashed it. The rush was like nothing else. I'd actually grown to adore the euphoria that came from blow. Then the self-hatred would make me lose the amazing high. Especially when I forced myself to acknowledge I was far worse than that kid. The one who'd killed my mother.

It was a vicious cycle.

But with José out of commission, it was up to me to make sure that Miguel wasn't getting screwed by his supplier. So, the cycle continued.

After I gave the all-clear that the hit I'd taken was pure snow, my associates and I exchanged the goods for a cash-filled briefcase. Never had I imagined that this was where I would end up when I dreamed of going undercover all those years ago. I didn't even recognize myself any longer. I'd moved up the ranks in the organization and was now third in command, right behind José Pérez. Álvarez had been hinting over the last couple of months that he wanted to begin grooming his punk ass nephew to take over for him when the time came.

When I first met Alejandro, he had more interest in sampling the merchandise than selling it. He was a spoiled little shit who did nothing but ride the white and spend his uncle's cash. Miguel just kept telling me the boy would grow up. I had my doubts.

Fifty-two minutes later, I pulled up to the security gate at the end of the driveway. Through the trees, I could just make out the top of the red roof of the house. An armed guard exited the small building to my left, a walkie-talkie in his hand. He spoke into it, advising the house I was here. Loud static and a scratchy voice spoke Spanish through the walkie, and the metal gate belched out a roar before it began rattling along the tracks to open up. I revved the bike before heading in. The second I crossed some invisible line, the metal gate began to close behind me.

I groaned when I spotted Alejandro's gunmetal Porsche 911 GT2 RS. The kid was clearly compensating for something by driving a car that cool. After dropping my kickstand and removing my helmet, I headed inside. I knew Miguel and Alejandro would be sitting in the courtyard in the center of the house. Like in Mexico, entire homes were built around a center courtyard where the family could visit. It also served as a security feature.

I weaved my way through the house, passing several armed men. I'd just reached the open French doors leading outside when a burst of husky, feminine laughter had me stopping in my tracks. The sound flowed through me and settled right in my gut, setting off warning signs. My feet started me moving forward again, but my steps were slower this time. Leaves and rocks crunched under my booted feet as I moved across the brick walk. My eyes scanned the area, and my whole body felt tight with an unknown tension.

I rounded the large tree that shaded about half the courtyard, and the first person I spotted was Miguel. Based on the files the D.E.A. had on him, I knew he was fifty-eight years old, although he appeared much younger. He had minimal flecks of gray in his pitch-black hair, and only a few age lines graced his face. His figure was trim. He really was in his prime. In fact, at this moment, wearing a pressed pair of khakis and baby blue polo, with a genuine smile on his face, I'd guess women would consider him good looking.

Across from him was Alejandro. The elder Álvarez was polished and almost debonair. The younger was a punk. He wore tattered jeans several sizes too big, cinched tightly at the waist with a giant belt. His oversized basketball jersey was tucked in at the front but then hung sloppily down to mid-thigh, and the gold chains around his neck were quintessential douchebag. Add in the aviator glasses and his whole persona screamed he was trying too hard.

"Tomás, welcome back. I assume there were no complications today." Miguel asked, his hand outstretched to shake mine.

"Yes, sir. Everything went as planned."

"Wonderful. You know Alejandro, of course. And this beautiful woman is Gabriela."

My vision was consumed with the woman who stepped forward, her arm looped through the man-child's next to her. Hair of varying shades of brown, from light to dark, was curled and fell down around her slender shoulders, a few tendrils cupping her perfectly sized breasts. She was absolutely stunning, and everything in me screamed *danger*.

She smiled at me, and there was a flash of a calculating look behind her chocolate brown eyes that disappeared quickly. A look that said she was sizing me up. Who was this woman and what was she doing with Alejandro?

I shook my head slightly when I realized Miguel had moved closer to me and was speaking low. Shit, I didn't need this distraction.

"I want you to take Alejandro to the club with you tonight and show him the lab."

Internally, I groaned. The dance club was a legitimate business, but it also housed a back room, the lab where some of Miguel's drug supply was cut. Considering the way his nephew spent money, I didn't think it was a great idea to give him unlimited access to a fuck-ton of pure drugs. If shit went missing, it was my ass on the line.

"*Tio*, we gotta get going, man. I promised to show Gabby a good time tonight." Alejandro practically whined.

Miguel waved him off good-naturedly. "Go, then, enjoy yourself."

His placating smile turned serious. "Remember, I want you to meet Tomás later this evening though. No excuses. This is *el negocio de la familia*, family business, and you need to make that a priority. Do you understand?"

Alejandro sighed like an over-dramatic teenager. "*Sí, tío. Yo te entiendo.* I understand."

My eyes tracked the couple as the man-child led his lady friend away. The green dress she wore hugged her curves, dipping in at the waist before flaring out over her hips. It barely covered her ass and her long, toned legs had my fingertips itching for a single touch. She hadn't spoken a word, and it had me intrigued, because she had absorbed the entire conversation around her.

What was she trying to learn?

CHAPTER 3

AFTER THAT FIRST NIGHT, Victor had negotiated a deal with Alejandro and Mikey, getting me on as a full-time dancer. And now that I was dating Alejandro, I was a frequent visitor to Miguel's home. Between there and *Sweet SINoritas*, I would have thought I'd have gotten some whiff of Ernesto, but I kept hitting dead end after dead end. I knew it wasn't like I was going to accidentally stumble across my missing brother in one of the bedrooms, but I was slowly losing hope.

Miguel was actually quite charming and attractive. I could see where his nephew got his looks. He could, however, learn a lot from his uncle about how to charm a woman. The man I'd met today, on the other hand, Tomás, was... rugged and harsh looking. His angular jaw was covered with two or three days' worth of growth, and his nose was slightly crooked. It was his piercing, almost-black eyes, set deep beneath prominent eyebrows that captured my attention though.

After his gaze had caught mine, I forced a smile to my face. He studied me like I'd studied him, only I knew it was happening. My skin tingled, even while alarm bells went off. He was something different.

Intense.

Brooding.

Intriguing.

Overly observant.

Definitely someone I needed to avoid.

I'd straightened my shoulders and kept watching him with a critical eye, trying to determine what it was about this man that didn't fit. When his eyes moved back to Miguel, I let out a breath I didn't realize I'd been holding. My fingers began to ache, and I discovered I'd clenched them in a fist. I wiggled them to get blood flowing again and then wiped my sweaty palms on my dress.

When Alejandro led me away, I resisted the temptation to look over my shoulder, but the hairs on the back of my neck stood on end, and the feeling of being observed by Tomás stayed with me long after we left the courtyard.

"Gabby, are you even listening to me?"

"*Sí, papi,*" I cooed, batting my lashes at Alejandro. He was easily led with only the tiniest bit of flirtation. I only had to smile and rub my boobs against his arm while I cuddled up close, and he practically ate out of my hand. It was almost embarrassing, really.

"What did I say then?" He asked, petulantly, shooting me a look.

I barely refrained from rolling my eyes. Lord, he was such a child. With four older brothers, I'd become an expert at half-listening to what men said and keeping up with the conversation. "You were telling me how excited you were that your uncle finally seems to be including you in more of the family business. This back room sounds interesting. Can I come with? See what it is you're doing? Maybe I can help you impress your uncle. Not that I think you need help. I bet you'll do amazing, *papi*." I patted his arm and smiled animatedly, beaming in fake pride. The more Alejandro knew about the family business, the better my chances of finding Ernesto. Every day, millions of secrets were spilled during pillow talk. The only problem was dreading said pillow talk.

"No, you can't come with me. Not tonight at least. Maybe some other time."

I pouted for effect. "Fine."

When we reached the Porsche, he opened my door for me. The first time he'd ever done such a thing. Maybe some of his uncle's charm was finally rubbing off on him?

I realized my mistake when he reached past me, opened the glove box, and pulled out a gun. Alejandro carrying a weapon made me nervous.

"What—" I unconsciously moved into a defensive pose, preparing to knock the firearm out of his hand if it became necessary, "—are you doing with a gun?"

I cursed inside my head when my question came out shakier than I expected. My shoulders sagged, and my racing heart skipped a beat before he did nothing but holster the weapon behind his back, under his baggy shirt. I remained guarded, even though the firearm was out of sight.

"I'm protecting what's mine." He puffed out his chest like a rooster showing off.

"Protection from what? We're on your uncle's property behind a secured gate."

Alejandro's expression was one I couldn't decipher. "You never know," he said, before striding around to his side of the vehicle. He stood at the open door, staring at me.

"Are you getting in or not?" he asked in a sharp tone, one eyebrow raised.

I slid into the passenger seat, still trying to figure out where this suddenly menacing behavior rose from. I remained silent the entire drive back to my house.

"I'll be back to pick you up at eight," he said before peeling away.

He didn't walk me to my door.

I'D BEEN HOME ABOUT TWENTY MINUTES WHEN A KNOCK sounded. I slipped the chain off to let Victor in.

"You okay?" He asked once inside.

"I told you I could handle things. You can't keep just dropping by. If Alejandro or any of his friends see you…" I trailed off.

Victor, normally the calm brother, ran his hands through his hair in frustration. "I fucking hate this."

I laid my hand on his arm. "I trust you to have my back. But you also have to trust that I know what I'm doing. Please."

He studied me in the sunlight streaming through the

front windows. Finally, he sighed. "You call me the second something doesn't feel right. Don't try to be a hero, Ines."

I kissed him on the cheek, let him out, locked the door, and slid the chain home.

I hadn't mentioned Tomás.

CHAPTER 4

WARM, scantily-clad bodies moved and gyrated on the dance floor, and the air was filled with the rhythmic beats of music blasting out of the speakers around the room. I lounged in the corner of the VIP section sipping a gin and tonic, impatiently waiting on Alejandro to arrive. I glared around the room, surveying the area for undercover cops trying to make a bust, as well as any of Miguel's enemies. I noticed several of his associates sprinkled around the VIP area, gorgeous women hanging on their arm. These were men whose goal was to make money and get power. My job was to take both of those things away.

On a second pass around the room, I spotted *her*.

Gabriela. I tracked her movements as she and Alejandro weaved in and out the crowd. Her dark-chocolate hair was pulled up in a ponytail that hung over her shoulder. Her skin was on display in the backless, curve-hugging dress she wore, which caused an interested twitch beneath my belt. I squashed the sensation even as I watched her hips shake to the music when they stopped for Alejandro to clasp hands and shoulder bump some of his friends.

"That's one hot piece of ass with our boy, eh *esé?*"

I turned to stare down Rico, who reclined in his chair, feet propped on the red plush ottoman in front of him. He coolly sipped his beer, gaze also locked on Gabriela. Irrational jealousy flared, which I quickly stamped out.

I shrugged. "Not my type."

Rico sent me a smirk before sipping his beer. "I hear you get to teach junior some of the family business tonight. I'm glad it's you on babysitting duty and not me."

Glad for the switch of topic, I shrugged again. "He's still young and more concerned with partying than business. Maybe he'll grow up soon, but it's doubtful."

"You better not let boss man hear you talk that way," Rico warned.

"I've expressed my concerns with Miguel. He thinks the kid will come around with patience and guidance." I took another sip of my watered-down drink, still observing the couple across the room.

"Still, better you than me."

Honestly, babysitting was better than some of the things I could be required to do. I sat up a little straighter when Alejandro leaned over to whisper in Gabriela's ear. She frowned at whatever he'd said, but gave a stiff nod in response.

It was my turn to scowl when he and his buddies moved away from her, leaving her standing there. *What the hell was so important that he left her alone?* I relaxed a few moments later when she smiled brightly and waved over another woman. They animatedly chatted before heading out to the dance floor.

I knew my attention should be on conversations going on around me so I could pass off intel to Landon, but my focus kept drifting back to the gorgeous woman laughing and rolling her hips to the music.

Distractions like her could get me killed.

I forced myself to move, to wander around and mingle with Miguel's associates. After ten minutes, and learning nothing that I didn't already know, I gave up. When I looked back out to the dance floor, it took a moment to locate Gabriela. Some drunken ass was harassing her. I watched as she attempted to blow him off, but he wasn't taking the hint. Without thinking, I stomped down the steps and through the crowd, elbowing my way past all the dancing couples. I ignored the dirty looks being shot my way, zeroing in on Gabriela.

When I stepped within earshot, I heard her bite out, "*Vete a la mierda.* How many languages do I need to speak for you to understand I'm not interested? Now, go away."

For a moment, I was both impressed and turned on. Who knew telling someone to fuck off would sound so sexy? My arousal swiftly switched to rage, though, when the inebriated piece of shit grabbed her arm, hard enough she winced.

"Let her go," I ground out, my fists clenched at my side in an effort not to punch the bastard.

Two sets of eyes shot in my direction. Relief flashed across her face while the jackass holding her arm sneered at me.

"This doesn't concern you, man."

I took another step forward, putting myself nose to nose with him. "If you don't take your hand off of her in the next two seconds, I'm going to break your fingers.

"One. Two."

I grabbed his free hand and snapped both his thumb and pinky outward, and felt the bones break. He roared and released his hold on Gabriela, cradling his now-broken digits to his chest.

I took the opportunity to gently push her behind me.

"Motherfucker, you broke them," he choked out.

I crossed my arms over my chest. "I don't make idle threats. Maybe next time you'll keep your fucking hands to yourself. Now get the hell out of here."

The man stared at us with hatred, and glanced around at the people watching the show. We'd attracted a crowd. He was either smart or sober enough to realize it was a mistake to engage any further. When he walked past us, still cradling his hand against his chest, he spat out, "*Puta.*"

I swept my arm out in front of Gabriela to block her lunge for the idiot, a growl erupting from her before she bit out, "*Bastardo.*"

He shot a glare at us over his shoulder but kept moving.

"I had things under control."

I huffed out a small laugh. "Yes, I could see that."

Gabriela crossed her arms over her chest. It took all my energy to keep my eyes locked with hers and not let my vision drift southward. "I did. He was seconds away from a knee to the nuts. He would have been writhing on the floor if you hadn't interfered."

"A knee to the nuts huh?" I smirked.

"I have brothers who taught me how to defend myself." Her voice was filled with pride.

"What's going on here?"

Alejandro and his buddies had returned. Where the hell had they been this whole time?

Just as I was about to lay into him for leaving his girlfriend alone, Gabriela spoke up.

"Nothing, *papi*. Tomás just asked Estelle to dance." She looped her arm through his, while her other hand went to his chest and began tracing imaginary lines back and forth with her finger.

I stared at the change that had come over her. Where minutes ago she'd been feisty and ready to unman some jerk, now she was simpering and submissive. Why the pretense? Why didn't she want Alejandro to know what had actually happened? He continued studying me, his body tense, but I remained impassive. Suddenly his muscles relaxed, and he broke out into a huge smile.

"It's about time you loosen up a little and enjoy yourself. You're always so uptight and serious, Tomás." He laughed and nudged one of his friends. My gaze, however, remained on Gabriela, whose eyes briefly darted over to meet mine before quickly re-focusing on Alejandro. I didn't know what the deal was with her, but I'd play along. For now.

I gave a small smile and shrugged. "What can I say. Sometimes all it takes is a beautiful woman."

Gabriela's friend, who'd been quietly standing off to the side, blushed at my words, even though we both knew this was a ruse.

I reached out to her. "How about that dance?"

She took two small steps forward and placed her hand in

mine, smiling a little uncertainly. I led her away from the group to the edge of the dance floor just as a Spanish love song began to play. I was a shit dancer, so we mostly just swayed back and forth, my arms awkwardly at her waist and her hands on my shoulders like we were in middle school.

"Thanks for what you did for Gabby back there," her voice was so soft I had to strain to hear her over the music.

Estelle was pretty. Her blonde hair hung limply down her back, and her blue eyes were set a little too close together, but she had a nice smile. She didn't set my blood on fire like her friend, though. A fire I needed to put out immediately. I couldn't afford to piss off Alejandro or Miguel.

"Not a problem. I do have a question though."

She peered up at me with caution in her gaze. Like she wasn't sure she should be answering my questions. I wondered if she was hiding something. If they both were.

When she remained silent, I took that as a sign to ask. "Why didn't Gabriela want Alejandro to know what happened just now?"

Estelle laughed, which entirely transformed her face from subtly pretty to beautiful. "You must not know a lot about women. We don't want our men to worry unnecessarily. If Alejandro had known that some man harassed her while he was gone, he would have been upset. He would have blamed himself that he hadn't been here to protect her. Also, he might be less inclined to leave her alone." She giggled nervously. "Not…not that she doesn't want to spend time with him, but no woman wants her man hovering over her constantly. Besides, Gabby really can take care of herself."

Every word she said made sense, but I wasn't buying it. Gabriela was too quick to shift gears.

I hated puzzles, but this was one I needed to solve.

After Estelle and I finished our dance, I excused myself and went in search of Alejandro. It was time to head to the back. I wanted to get this over with. When I finally found him, he and his idiot compadres were downing shots in the VIP section, pointedly ignoring Gabriela, who sat at his side looking bored.

"Alejandro," I called out with impatience. "It's time to go."

Initially I thought he was going to ignore me, but eventually he rose from the table. He bent down and spoke to Gabriela, but I couldn't hear what he said over the music. He grabbed her ponytail, yanking her head back. His mouth slammed down on hers and I could see his tongue sloppily shoved into her mouth. A display of ownership. I resisted the urge to tear him away from her, and plastered a bored expression on my face when I caught him watching me out of the corner of his eye. After what felt like hours, he tore his mouth from hers, straightened, and strode toward me, wiping the corner of his mouth with his thumb and then sucking the moisture off it. When he was even with me, I ignored the smirk he sent my way, turned, and walked toward the back of the club.

All the while, I was fighting the urge to beat the little fucker within an inch of his life.

CHAPTER 5

I TOOK a large swallow of my nearby water, hoping to wash Alejandro's spit from my mouth. This was the part of the job I despised. Letting him paw at me. It was also the first time he'd shown such aggression. I'd been in so much shock I couldn't do more than let him ravage my mouth. I winced when I rubbed my head where he'd pulled my hair. That kiss had been a show of possession strictly for Tomás' bene-fit. It cemented the fact Alejandro hadn't believed my story about him wanting to dance with Estelle, who I needed to go find. She'd told me she'd stick around.

From my higher vantage point, I was able to scan the room more easily than if I were at floor level. It only took me a moment before I spotted her. I waited a minute or two, and when it looked like she was looking in my direc-tion, I waved to try and get her attention. When she spotted me, she hurried over. I pulled her to a corner table where our backs were to the wall so we could talk without fear of someone eavesdropping.

"Tell me about your dance with Tomás."

Estelle knew what I really wanted to know. Her smiling face belied the caution in her eyes as she glanced around to make sure we were alone. "Your Tomás is awfully inquisitive."

My heartbeat sped up. My eyes widened, and I nodded for her to continue.

"He wanted to know how we knew each other, how long we'd been friends. He also wanted to know why you didn't wish Alejandro to be privy to the little confrontation that happened earlier."

Damn it. "And? What did you tell him?"

Estelle shifted a little nervously in her chair, which had me just a tad twitchy. I trusted her with my life, but she wasn't a professional. She was my best friend. I knew it wasn't the smartest idea to have someone from my real life near me, but I needed that connection. Estelle was the logical choice as my lifeline to the outside world, because she was a woman. Alejandro wouldn't be threatened by our relationship. To him, women were nothing more than arm candy. Misogyny at its finest. I did my best to keep her away from this side of my life, so we only saw each other on occasion, and only here at the club. I didn't go to her house, and she didn't come to mine.

Victor was keeping watch over her. I wished they could see what I saw when they were together, but both of them were too stubborn to realize they were in love with each other.

"I said the first thing that came to mind. Women don't like their men to worry over them and since he'd already handled it, there wasn't any point. It would only make Alejandro overprotective and hover."

I was actually impressed, because it was totally legit. Of course, it wasn't the real reason. My goal was to appear timid, sheltered. Like violence didn't exist in my world. I needed to appear harmless and innocent so Alejandro would drop his guard. It was my way of trying to gain information to find my brother. I'd had zero luck so far.

When we'd first started dating, I overheard him talking on the phone one day about someone I thought could have been my brother, but when he noticed I was listening, he went into the other room and closed the door. Since then though, I'd kept my head down and my ears open. I must have been playing my role well enough, because more often than not, he conducted business in front of me. Recently, I'd been hearing him talk about something big that was going down soon, but I hadn't been able to figure out what he was talking about. I always made sure it seemed like I wasn't paying attention in hopes he'd spill.

"Do you think he believed you?"

Estelle shrugged. "I don't know. He had this look on his face. Like he smelled the bullshit I was spouting. But, he didn't press for more, so maybe. I wish I had a better answer for you."

I put my hand on hers and squeezed. "He either believed you or he didn't. There's nothing either of us can do now. Thanks for being here. I'd be lost without you."

Alejandro would be gone for the rest of the night, so it was time for me to head home.

Once I was back in my apartment, I unscrewed the vent off the wall in the second bedroom and pulled out a burner phone hidden inside. I took it into my bathroom and turned on the shower. A few rings later, a man answered.

"Did you learn anything tonight?" The voice on the other end questioned.

"Nothing pertaining to Ernesto. I did hear about a drug exchange taking place tomorrow night at a truck stop off Interstate 90, about ten miles from Gary. I don't know exactly where, though."

I hated that I had nothing more to offer, but every little bit of intel I passed on that stopped the trafficking of drugs through Chicago was still a positive.

"*Estoy orgulloso de ti, conejita.*" I'm proud of you, little bunny.

I smiled at the nickname, though it almost had me in tears. I knew he was proud of me, but I felt like a failure. What if I never found Ernesto? I knew others on the force were looking for him without success, but it weighed heavily on me. I missed my father and brothers.

"*Te amo papá. Buenas noches..*" I disconnected the call, wishing I could have spoken longer, but we both knew our calls needed to be short. I turned off the phone and then the water before returning to the bedroom and replacing the phone behind the vent.

I quickly changed into my pajamas and crawled under the covers. While I waited for sleep to come, my thoughts returned to the club and how quickly Tomás broke that idiot's fingers. I hadn't lied when I said my brothers taught me how to protect myself. If one of them had done what he had, I would have been pissed at their interference. Except with Tomás, I found it incredibly hot. Watching him grab that guys hand and snap his fingers, as horrifying as it may sound, totally turned me on.

I'd been looking at him in a way that was going to get me in trouble. And considering the questions he was asking, it was more important than ever that I avoid him.

CHAPTER 6

LOCKING THE BIKE, I stowed my helmet and took a deep breath. I both hated and loved coming here. I strode up the walk and pressed the button on the front door. A raucous buzzing sounded before the lock on the door disengaged, allowing me to open it. Once it was closed behind me, the lock reengaged. The twelve-foot ceilings caused my footfalls to echo as I strode down the white ceramic-tiled hallway, which was more of a lengthy foyer. When I reached the desk in the middle of a grand room, I was greeted by the elderly, gray-haired woman behind it.

"Mr. Thomas, welcome back. It's so good to see you again." Her smile was warm, welcoming, and far too familiar.

"Hi Mary. Is he available?" I asked in a tone that I prayed conveyed hope and not dread.

She glanced down at her calendar and back up at me, the smile still in place. "You're in luck. Group is just about to recess for the afternoon. Preston should be out in a few minutes, if you'd like to take a seat."

I nodded my thanks and took a seat in the plush burgundy office chair. My foot tapped out a staccato of restlessness while I waited. Every time I came here, the urge to never return became stronger, but I knew if I didn't, I'd regret it. Besides, I didn't come here for me.

"Hello, Brody."

My head shot up at the voice, and I locked eyes with a younger version of me. He wore blue jeans and a red-and-blue plaid button-down shirt, the cuffs undone and sleeves rolled up to expose his forearms and the track marks peppering them.

I stood awkwardly, never knowing if I should shake hands with or hug him. Choosing the former, I discretely wiped my palm on my pant leg before reaching out to grasp his hand. I could tell my choice disappointed him.

"Preston." My voice came out crisper than usual.

"Do—" he cleared the roughness from his throat, "—do you want to step outside for some air?"

I nodded and waited for him to lead the way. We strode through the grand room and out a side sliding glass door into the gardens. The sounds of birds chirping and the faint hint of water flowing were heard. It was meant to be soothing, but only served as a reminder of where I was. We continued walking in silence until we reached a park bench under a giant tree. Preston sat at one end and I claimed the other, both of us staring straight ahead.

"Have you been to see her?" He asked after a moment, his voice soft and hesitant.

I cleared my throat. "I was going there next."

"You know her birthday is coming up, right?" His laugh was humorless. "Never mind, of course you do."

I ignored the last. I finally turned toward the near-stranger sitting next to me. "So, how have things been going?"

He shrugged. "Oh, you know, the usual. I wake up, eat breakfast, go to individual counseling, then group therapy, eat lunch, maybe take a shit during my free time, have more therapy, work out in the gym, eat dinner, another group discussion, and then I jack off before bed. Rinse. Repeat."

"Why do you do this every time?" My jaw clenched while I tried to control the anger in my voice. "You ask about her, and then you get defensive and turn into an asshole. Don't get pissy with me because you're here. We both know you have a choice."

Preston spun sharply in my direction, jabbing his finger in my direction. "Screw you, Brody. Don't try to act like you're better than me. You're only here to show everyone what a good person you are by supporting your addict brother. We both know that's the reason you keep coming, so don't bother denying it. You're a judgmental asshole."

He jumped up and stomped in the direction of the building, fists clenched at his side.

"Damn it, Preston, wait," I called, following behind him.

He spun around so quickly, I almost collided with him. "You know what? I think it's time you stop coming. Like you said, we do this every time. You're bitter and angry." He held up his hand to stop me when I opened my mouth. "No. You are, Brody. And I get it. I really do. If our roles were reversed, I'd feel the same way. But we can't keep doing this. Every time you come, I pray for a different outcome, but it never changes. It's not good for either one of us. You show up full of resentment, and then I feel guilty all over again, which makes me want to use to numb it. She's dead. I killed her, and there's nothing I can do to change that."

His shoulders drooped with the weight of the burden I knew he carried. Me showing up only made it heavier. Deep down, I knew that, but I tortured us both anyway. I *wanted* his guilt. I resented my brother. Sometimes, I even hated him for what he'd done. Then I hated myself even more, because I was a far worse person than Preston would ever be.

It was why I'd joined the D.E.A., why I'd gone undercover. I wanted to rid the streets of the drugs that had destroyed my family. It had become my life's goal. My obsession even. Because if it weren't for my brother's heroin addiction, our mother would still be alive.

"You're right, and I'm sorry." My tone was heavy with regret. "I don't want to fight every time I come. And maybe I *should* stop coming. The thing is, I don't know if I can. You're my baby brother, Preston. We're family. Our whole lives, mom taught us that we only had each other to rely on. Us Thomases look after one another. You're all I have left, and I love you."

Preston swallowed hard and stared at the ground for a long moment. When his eyes returned to mine, a sheen covered them. When he blinked, it disappeared. "I love you too, Brody, but this is too damn hard. I think we're both better off if you just forgot I was here. So, please, for your sake, if not mine…don't come back."

He turned his back to me again, and with a straight spine and his head high, my brother walked away.

This time, I let him go.

CHAPTER 7

SMOKY EYES STARED BACK at me from the reflection in the mirror. I'd almost finished my makeup, and soon my street clothes would come off and I'd slip into a purple lace bra, matching g-string, and mile-high stilettos that I prayed nightly I didn't break my ankle wearing. I listened to the girls' chatter while they too got ready for the evening's performances. When Ernesto had first gone missing, I thought going undercover as a stripper was perfect. It gave me the opportunity to get close to Miguel Álvarez and his associates to try and find my brother. Now, weeks later, after dancing with men ogling, propositioning, and occasionally groping me, I dreaded it. In fact, it made me heartsick for so many reasons.

A lot of these women had no choice. Granted, there were a couple who danced to either pay for college or to pay off student loans. It was their body, they could do whatever they wanted with it.

It was the women who had no education and no other

options that bothered me. Michele, for instance, was here because she became pregnant at the age of fifteen. Her rich family and their equally rich friends all abandoned her when they found out. With nowhere to go, she was forced to drop out of school. After living on the streets until the baby was born, Michele moved into a women's shelter. She survived the first year on government assistance, but she wanted more for her and her baby. With the help of a fake ID, she began dancing here about a year ago. In that time, she'd earned enough to move into her own apartment, start classes at the local community college, and pay for daycare for her little girl. Michele was a sweet kid, and I hated using her like I was.

"Hey girl!"

I swiveled in my seat to see her strolling toward me through the sea of half-naked women milling around the room. She hugged me and air-kissed my cheek so she didn't ruin our makeup.

"Hi yourself. How's Maisy?" I pasted on the smile I practiced daily to look sincere.

"Oh my god, she's hitting her terrible twos, and they sure didn't lie with that description. I feel horrible for even saying this, but she's become a complete asshole. Tantrums galore. Makes me want to either tear my hair out or cry right along with her. Everything is 'no'. There's no middle ground. It's her way or 'no'. Of course, when it's not her way...melt down city."

I couldn't help but laugh. "I know exactly what you mean. My niece was the same way at that age. Thankfully, she'll outgrow it. You just have to put up with it until then."

Michele sighed dramatically, her expression woeful. "I

only hope we both survive until then. My patience is hanging on by a thread. They need to give every teenage girl a two-year-old to babysit twenty-four hours a day for a week. Best birth control ever.

"Anyway, how are things between you and Alejandro? You guys seem hot and heavy. I'm so jealous. I wish I had a man who worshipped me like he does you."

Inwardly, I cringed, because her assessment wasn't too far off. Alejandro did seem overly attached. "He does treat me like a queen. I've never had that before. I keep waiting for him to realize I'm not good enough, like my last boyfriend did. I mean, I take off my clothes in front of men for a living. I love the money, but—" I shrugged, "I never pictured this for myself. Either way, until Alejandro smartens up, I'm going to keep hoping it works out between us."

Michele gasped. "Girl, don't you ever think you're not good enough for someone. We all do this for one reason or another. I don't give a shit what anyone thinks of me. You shouldn't either. At least you're not selling your body like some of these catty bitches. Or high on dope just to make it through your set. There are worse things you could be doing with your life."

I hugged her with sincerity. "Thank you for being such a good friend."

Michele flushed and waved me away. She looked around before lowering her voice to a whisper. "Did you hear the rumor going around? About the cop?"

Instantly, I perked up and leaned in closer. "Oh my god, you have to tell me."

"Well, from the sounds of it, someone who works for

Mr. Álvarez caught some cop snooping around. Word is they plan on killing him."

I suddenly found myself unable to draw in a breath. Black spots danced in my vision, and there was a loud buzzing in my ears. Michele's worried face appeared fuzzy. I could see her mouth moving, but I couldn't hear a word she was saying. Slowly, I pulled myself together, and the buzzing sound began to fade until only a small *whoosh*ing sound remained.

I shook my head to clear it and rubbed my forehead. "I'm so sorry, I don't know what happened."

"Are you sure you're okay?"

Pasting on a fake smile, I waved off her question. "I'm fine, really. Whatever it was, it's gone. Didn't mean to freak you out."

Michele still looked like she wanted to ask more questions, but she let it go. "Anyway, I don't know how accurate the rumor is or anything. I mean, I know Mr. Álvarez isn't entirely on the up and up, I mean, no one who makes the kind of money be obviously does is, but to kill a police officer?"

My laugh came out awkward and shaky. "Yeah, that seems a little extreme."

I was desperate for more information, but I didn't want to appear too eager. "Crap, I need to finish getting ready. Mikey will kill me if I'm late. I'll see you out there, okay?"

Michele nodded. "You got it. Knock their socks off out there."

She smiled and waved. I took a few deep breaths, trying to get my focus back. I didn't need to do anything to fuck it

up. I ignored my churning stomach and I pushed out of my
mind all the scenarios in which I found my brother dead.

CHAPTER 8

THE MINUTE I walked in the door of *Sweet SINoritas*, which I thought was a ridiculous play on words, the subtle smell of sex filled my nose. Technically, the women who danced here weren't allowed to have sex with the clientele, however, everyone knew it happened. The manager, Mikey, got a cut of the girl's fee, so they didn't do a lot to curb the behavior.

I strode through the dimly-lit room toward the bar, constantly observing my surroundings. The sounds of *Pony* by Ginuwine screamed from the speakers. I barely controlled myself from groaning at the cliché.

"Tomás, look at you, slumming it with us down here in the gutters. I thought you were living it big up there with Mr. Álvarez?"

Mikey "The Shark" Martinez stepped out from behind the bar to greet me, hand outstretched, a smarmy smile gracing his face. A smile I didn't return. He reminded me less of a shark and more of a bulldog. His face and nose were flattened and his head was large for his body, which was tall and stocky. He was also a sketchy fucker. Which was why I was here. Rumor had it he was skimming money off the top of his drug sales. I'd come here to remind him of the consequences of stealing from Miguel Álvarez.

"Why don't you and I have a tête-à-tête somewhere a little more private." I ignored his gesture, which forced him to awkwardly drop his hand to his side, and his smile dimmed.

"Pri—" He cleared his throat, swallowing hard, before rubbing his ear as he stuttered. "—privately?"

I jerked my head in the direction of his office. "Lead the way, Mikey."

Keeping an eye on the various bouncers who observed us, I followed him to a red velvet covered door marked PRIVATE. I closed the door behind me and moved against the far wall, making sure my back was to it so I had full view of the room, including the door we'd just entered.

"Why don't you have a seat." I gestured to the only chair, which was positioned behind the desk.

Hesitantly, he seated himself and, in a surprisingly smart move, kept his hands where I could see them. Slowly, I strode toward him, stepping behind him, where I stopped. He shifted in his chair, and sweat beaded across his forehead.

I laid my hands on his shoulders. He flinched at the contact. "Do you know why I'm here?"

Mikey cleared his throat. "I swear I planned on paying Mr. Álvarez back. I just needed a little extra to get by."

I sighed heavily in disappointment. "Mikey, Mikey, Mikey. I like you. I really do. Which is why I'd hoped those rumors I'd been hearing weren't true."

He started to turn, but I shoved him back down in the chair. "Tomás, please."

I leaned down and spoke low in his ear. "You know what happens to people who 'borrow' money from Mr. Álvarez, don't you, Mikey?"

He trembled beneath my fingertips, and uttered only a single word. "Please."

I stood upright and gave his shoulder a light slap before removing my hands and moving around to tower over him. I placed my hands on the crappy particle board desk and invaded his personal space. I tried not to gag at the smell of stale coffee and cigarettes.

"My reason for being here was to determine whether the rumor was true or not. I don't know how much money you took. I don't even care. I'm showing you a professional courtesy. This is your single warning. You have one hour to return what you've stolen and you'll live to tell your kids about it. You'll likely have a few less fingers, but at least you'll be alive. One hour. Then I'll be passing along your indiscretion to Mr. Álvarez. We both know he isn't known for his kindness or his leniency. There's one rule. You don't fuck with his money or his drugs."

His voice was shaky. "What happens if I can't? I mean, what if I need more time?"

"There is no more time. If it's going to take you more than an hour, then you better spend that time with your family telling them you love them. Either you'll be dead, or they will be. All depends on Miguel's mood. He's capricious, you know."

I turned and strode to the door. I stood in the now-open

doorway and looked back at Mikey, who remained frozen in place. "I'll be at the bar waiting. Don't fuck this up."

I made my way to the bar without incident. Not that I expected Mikey to try anything, but desperate people did desperate things. After sidling up to the large, smooth mahogany bar, I ordered my usual gin and tonic. I watched as several women led a client to a private room where whatever arrangements they'd made would be performed. Already, I was bored. The currently playing song finished and the dancer left the stage. When the music began again, I straightened, surprised by the haunting tones that floated around the room.

I didn't recognize the song, but it was certainly a strange choice to strip to. When the dancer stepped on the stage, all the saliva in my mouth dried up. *Holy fuck.*

Gabriela.

Her lithe body was meant to be worshipped. Perfect tits were shamefully covered by a barely-there bra. Her toned and tanned legs were meant to be wrapped around my waist. The scrap of fabric covering her pussy was useless since it did nothing to keep her covered. I swallowed hard.

She swayed and dipped and what should have been odd, considering the song choice, was instead sensual and erotic. My feet moved of their own accord, and I prowled toward the stage.

I knew the instant she spotted me, because her movements hiccupped. She recovered quickly, though.

I remained off to the side, standing in the shadows like a creepy Peeping Tom, though the object of my voyeurism was well aware I watched. When the tempo of the song changed, her movements followed suit. More than once

Gabriela's eyes met mine, and there were brief moments when I imagined she danced only for me. Finally, god had mercy on me because the song came to an end, and she hastily picked up stray bills that had fallen to the floor before exiting off the stage. I tracked her as she rounded the stage, now empty-handed. She flitted from table to table, flirting and smiling at the various suit-clad men seated nearest the stage. She avoided my gaze entirely.

I vacated my spot and decided it was time to reposition myself at the bar, which so happened to be where Gabriela now stood.

"Interesting song choice." Her breath caught and then quickly restarted. I casually leaned sideways against the bar with my ankles crossed.

She threw a half-hearted smile in my direction while she tried to shift further away from me. "Thanks."

I studied her while she pointedly ignored me. She gave off sultry siren vibes, but there was an air of innocence around her. What was her story? Fucking puzzles. It was time to see if I could get some answers.

CHAPTER 9

WHEN I'D SPOTTED Tomás watching me dance, I almost froze but forced myself to keep going. I couldn't help the occasional glances in his direction. His black t-shirt hugged his muscular body to perfection, while the tight blue jeans he wore hung low on his hips and accentuated the fact the man had zero fat around his waist. I couldn't see them, but somehow I knew his abs were rock-hard. Even standing in the shadows, his hawk-like gaze made my body heat.

My *abuela* would tell me it was fate that kept throwing him in my direction.

There was an intensity about him that was intriguing and mysterious, but that was Ines' hormones talking. The rational and focused Ines, on the other hand, knew any distraction from finding Ernesto was bad news. For so many reasons. Not the least of which was that it was dangerous to piss off your boyfriend. Even if the relationship was merely a ploy to gain information. So, no matter how attracted I was to Tomás, I had to constantly remind myself that *he was a member of the cartel.* Maybe if I kept repeating it to myself, it would sink in.

Forcing myself to ignore the man standing far too close, and the fact that I was practically naked, I called out to Damon, who was working behind the bar. "I need two vodka martinis, neat with three olives, a whiskey on the rocks, and a Corona without a lime, please."

I was acutely aware of Tomás' presence next to me, and it was driving me crazy. *He* was driving me crazy. "Stop staring at me. It's creepy as fuck."

He didn't even blink. Instead, he only gave me this cocky half-smile. Like he knew what he was doing to me and enjoyed it. *Asshole.*

"Sorry." He sounded anything but.

"I don't think Alejandro would appreciate you making a play for his woman."

He shrugged. "Who said I was making a play? Can't a man just appreciate a woman's beauty without trying to get into her pants?"

"Well, it sure seems like you're doing something with all the lurking in dark corners and well…the lurking."

This evoked an actual full-bodied laugh. *Holy shit, the man was absolutely breathtaking.* I shook the thought away. Damon chose that moment to arrive with the drinks.

"Look, I need to deliver these and get back to work. While you, in the meantime, need to stop being creepy." I grabbed a small serving tray from the end of the bar and placed the drinks, along with some napkins, on it. I picked it up and gave one last glance at the far too sexy Tomás before starting back toward the gentlemen's table who'd ordered the drinks.

"See you around, *raya.*"

I stumbled at the nickname and the promise in his words. *Shit.* Finding my footing again, I kept my eyes ahead and pasted on my fake smile before delivering the drinks I carried. It took everything in me to pay attention to what I was doing when all I could feel was Tomás eyes burning a hole in my back. My body was on alert. It also betrayed me, as my nipples pebbled and my core throbbed.

He knew exactly what he was doing do me.

A short time later, I saw Mikey approach him, fear pouring from the former. I couldn't get a gauge on what Tomás was feeling. They both moved from the bar and headed toward the office before disappearing inside. My focus alternated between serving drinks, avoiding straying hands, and observing that closed door, wondering what was going on behind it. I shivered with something like dread.

FIVE LONG HOURS LATER, MY FEET WERE SCREAMING IN AGONY and my ass was bruised from the pinches and light smacks I'd endured. I was also frustrated. None of the conversations I'd heard tonight were useful. No mention of a cop at all. It had me wondering if the rumor Michele heard was, in fact, just a rumor. I made a mental note to call my dad first thing in the morning. Now, all I wanted to do was take a shower, put my pajamas on, soak my feet in Epsom salt while I ate a pint of ice cream, and then crawl into my warm, comfortable bed.

"You about ready, Gabby?" Michele called out from the dressing room door.

"Yeah, give me just a sec."

I shut my locker and grabbed my bag, taking a quick look around to make sure I hadn't forgotten anything. Then I went to meet Michele.

"Soooo," she dragged out the word once we were outside and walking toward the train station. "Who was the hottie that was totally eye-fucking you half the night?"

Her eyes were lit with excitement and curiosity and she practically danced with giddiness waiting for my response.

"C'mon Gabby, spill it! He was dreamy." She sighed the last.

I shrugged. "He's just some guy who works for Mr. Álvarez. I don't even know him, really."

She shot me a look of disbelief. "You may not know him, but he sure as hell wants to know you."

"Well, it doesn't matter what he wants. I'm with Alejandro."

Michele snorted and rolled her eyes. "Pffft. Alejandro is a boy. Mr. Sexy is pure man."

"I don't think I've ever been called Mr. Sexy before."

We both screeched and spun toward the voice behind us, me instinctively ready to defend us.

"You…asshole," I stuttered out the insult, my fists curled at my sides in a defensive pose.

"Tsk, tsk *raya*. That wasn't very nice. Personally, I prefer Mr. Sexy." Tomás winked at Michele, who giggled like the eighteen-year-old she was.

I wondered at the change in him. The first time we'd met, he was this tense, serious man who oozed danger. Suddenly, he's flirty and charming. I didn't get it.

"What are you doing following us? I thought we agreed

you'd stop being creepy. Sneaking up on us and trying to scare the shit out of us definitely constitutes creepy. Do I need to call the cops?" I asked, crossing my arms over my chest and tapping my foot.

"Gabby!" Michele scolded.

Tomás just sent me that mysterious half-smile. I was beginning to really hate that smile, because I knew he was laughing at me.

"I saw you two lovely ladies walking alone, and I wanted to make sure you arrived at your destination safe and sound. You never know what kind of riff-raff might be lurking around here." His innocent expression didn't fool me.

"Oooh, that is so nice of you, Mr..." Michele batted her eyes even while she fished for information.

The smile he sent her was genuine, unlike the ones he flashed at me. "You can call me Tomás. Or Mr. Sexy. Whichever you prefer."

"It's nice to meet you—" she hesitated as though debating on which name to use. "—Tomás."

I almost let out a sigh of relief. I hated this feeling that was building inside me at their flirty banter. I'd swear it reeked of jealousy. And there was no way I was jealous over Tomás flirting with my friend. No way. I tried to bring Alejandro's face to mind, but the vision eluded me. All I could see was dark brown compelling eyes, windswept black hair, and thick, sensual lips that even now taunted me with that smile. *Shit.*

"As you can see, we're perfectly fine," I bit out, adding my own fake smile.

"Why don't I walk you ladies to your stop? You know, just to be safe and all." Tomás argued.

I waved him away, my smile even tighter now. "Oh, I wouldn't want to take you away from your important business. I'm sure Mr. Álvarez needs you to oversee some drug deal or another."

Beside me, Michele gasped.

Tomás' smile slowly flattened, and it was replaced with something almost like disappointment. The silence grew heavy until he cleared his throat.

"Well, since it's obvious my presence is both unwarranted and unwanted, I'll leave you ladies to continue on without me then. Have a good night." He offered a mock salute before turning on his heels and striding away.

"Oh my god, Gabby, what is wrong with you?" Michele harrumphed and stomped off in disgust.

"Michele, wait," I chased after, catching up with a few steps.

She kept walking, ignoring me entirely, even when we reached our stop at the el to wait for the train to arrive.

"Will you please look at me?" I begged. "I'm sorry, okay? I was rude to him and he didn't deserve it."

"No, he didn't. That's not even the entire reason I'm mad. I thought we were friends, and you lied to me."

"What are you talking about?" Had I inadvertently blown my cover somehow?

Michele pouted. "You told me you didn't really know him. There is something going on between you two. You could have just told me you didn't want to talk about him. You didn't have to lie to me. I hate being lied to."

"Michele, I'm sorry. I didn't intentionally lie to you okay."

There was nothing else I could say, so I waited. Finally, she relaxed and sighed. "I know you think I'm being over-dramatic, but there is nothing I despise more than being lied to. I'm sorry for overreacting."

I wasn't normally a touchy-feely person, and even as I reminded myself I was undercover, I hugged her.

"Friends still?"

She nodded. "Friends."

CHAPTER 10

FUCKING MIKEY. When I'd re-entered his office last night and he'd told me he was going to be ten gees short, I was livid. I knew what happened to people who fucked over Miguel. Because dope dealers were easily replaceable, he didn't hesitate to get rid of those who stole from him. I didn't know how to protect Mikey, and although I didn't condone what he did, he didn't deserve to die for his stupidity. I certainly didn't need more blood on my hands.

When my phone rang, I knew the night was about to get longer.

"This is Tomás."

"You're needed at the warehouse in the Fulton District." The disembodied voice commanded and then the line went dead.

Shit. Fulton meant someone was being "questioned." I turned the bike around and headed that way. Once there, I cut the lights and engine and rolled to a stop outside the building. I rapped out a series of knocks before the door cracked open. The light from behind the man at the door momentarily blinded me before my vision cleared and I recognized Javier. He let me in before closing the door behind me. We strode across the cement floor to a steel door on the far side of the room.

On the other side, a beaten and bloodied man sat strapped to a chair. His arms were tied behind him and each of his ankles were tied to the front legs of the chair. He was naked from the waist up and his chest was covered with blood. I wasn't sure if it was from wounds sustained to his chest or from what was dripping out of his mouth. Next to him was a table with a metal tray covered with various implements. I winced when I spotted a couple teeth.

"Welcome to the party."

I turned to see a giant of a man step out of the bathroom wiping his hands on a towel. Paulo Hernandez was six and a half feet of pure muscle and reminded me of a professional wrestler. He wore tailored Armani suits, kept a closely shaven mustache and goatee, and wore his shoulder-length, pitch black hair slicked back in a smooth ponytail. Not even a strand dared to stray its confinement. The single diamond in his ear sparkled in the lighting.

"Looks like you started without me. Who is he?" I didn't begin to believe that I knew all of the dealers who worked for Álvarez, but even beaten, he didn't strike me as one of them.

"Un *puerco estúpido.*" Paulo spat. *A stupid pig.*

Fuck. By the looks of things, he wasn't going to make it out of here alive.

"*¿Estas loco? ¿Porque mierda trajiste a un policía aquí?* Are you out of your mind? Why the fuck would you bring a cop here?"

Paulo shrugged. "Officer Rodriguez has been looking into a cleanup that could potentially lead back to Mr. Álvarez. I brought him here to discover what exactly he knows."

"How long has he been here, and what have you learned?"

"This is day number three without learning a goddamn thing except his name. The pig won't talk." I sensed the frustration, and perhaps even a little respect, in his voice. It didn't matter though, because everyone in this room knew he was going to die tonight.

"That's difficult to do when your mouth is full of blood." I dead-panned. "Besides, torture seldom leads to answers when the victim—especially a *cop* you stupid fuck—knows you're going to kill them anyway."

Paulo's fists clenched at my insult. I didn't give a shit. They'd called me here for a reason. Not the least of which, I was a step above them on the food chain. I was here because these two dipshits knew they'd fucked up. Paulo was a stupid fuck, but even he wasn't going to kill a cop investigating Miguel without notifying José or me. Jesus, what a fucking mess.

Miguel paid a shit ton of money to one of the best defensive legal teams in the entire tristate area. Crimes frequently "potentially led" to Álvarez. So far, nothing had stuck. An undercover cop was nothing new. It could have been handled. Now, unless I performed a goddamn miracle, he was a dead cop.

"Why don't you two step outside and leave me with Officer Rodriguez here."

I sensed Paulo's reluctance, but I didn't give a fuck. Javier nudged his arm and nodded his head in the direction of the door. They closed it behind them.

Even the sight of my knife didn't cause him to rear back in fear. Damn, the man was a brave mother fucker. I moved behind him and cut away the bindings around his wrists. He rubbed them in an attempt to ease the rope burn and stimulate circulation.

I squatted in front of him. "What I'm about to tell you will get me killed."

Not even so much as a blink. Forging ahead anyway, I spilled my secret.

"My name is Brody Thomas, and I'm an undercover D.E.A. agent. I'm being honest here when I tell you I don't know what to do to get you out of here alive."

Rodriguez turned his head before spitting out a mouth full of blood. "There's nothing you can do."

His voice was calm, resigned. My head dropped in defeat. Fuck. I wanted to scream in rage. To punch something. Because he was right.

"Actually, that's not true."

My head snapped back up at his words, hope brewing inside me. "What is it?"

"I need you to protect my sister."

I stared at him blankly. What the hell was he talking about? I opened my mouth to question him, but he continued. "My sister will come looking for me, if she hasn't already." He smiled, his front teeth missing, blood still filling his mouth. His eyes finally met mine. "Our dad was a cop. My brothers as well." He paused. "She's a bulldog. Scrappy and tenacious. Stubborn as hell. My brothers will have her six. But they all knew the case I was working on. Ines has probably already found a way in. Which means she needs someone else on the inside to keep her safe. That, Brody Thomas, is what you can do for me."

Before I could respond, the steel door behind me slammed open. I pivoted on the balls of my feet, gun in hand.

"Did you get anything?"

"No, nothing."

"Time for negotiations is over." He pulled out his gun. "He's not gonna talk."

I waited for Rodriguez to say something to contradict Paulo, but he just nodded his head in resignation. Even in the face of death, he remained calm and composed. His eyes remained fixed on mine, silently reminding me of his last request. And although I knew it was coming, I still flinched at the sound of the bullet exiting the chamber.

CHAPTER 11

THE KNOCK on the door surprised me. I groaned when I looked through the peephole and saw who was standing on the other side. I'd finally stopped thinking of him, and here he was again, in the flesh. "For god's sake. Why can't you just leave me alone?" I demanded when I flung the door open. Anger was better than arousal.

"Can I come in?" Tomás asked gravely.

I didn't know what to make of his attitude. He wasn't smug, snarky, or even flirty like all the previous times I'd seen him. There was a seriousness to him that made me both curious and nervous. Curiosity won out. I opened the door further and backed away, giving him room to enter.

"Come on in and have a seat. Can I get you something to drink? Water? Beer?"

He shook his head as he stepped past me. "No, thanks, I'm fine."

My already small apartment suddenly felt tiny with Tomás inside. I studied him. He had dark circles under his eyes, and his hair was mussed, like he'd been running his fingers through it. "Why don't you have a seat and tell me why you're here."

I made my way to the couch and settled in, waiting for him to do the same. There was a tension surrounding him. Finally, he took a seat, but avoided meeting my gaze.

After several moments of silence he finally looked at me. There was so much grief and sorrow in his eyes, I didn't want to hear whatever it was he had to say.

"I'm sorry, Ines."

I blinked several times before it processed that he'd said my name. My real name. *Shit.* Instead of panicking, I tried to laugh him off. "My name is Gabriela."

He didn't laugh with me.

"Your name is Ines Rodriguez."

Sweat trickled between my breasts, and I swallowed hard. Tomás was a member of the cartel, and now they knew who I was. "I think it might be time for you to leave."

I made my way towards the door. My hand had just touched the knob when his next words froze the blood in my veins.

"Ernesto Rodriguez."

I closed my eyes and waited for the bullet. When it didn't come, I turned to face my enemy.

"What did you say?" My voice came out on a whisper. Then, I remembered his first words to me. *I'm sorry.*

"You heard me Ines. I know who you are. I also know you've been looking for your brother."

On auto-pilot, I moved back to the couch and perched on the edge of my seat. Tomás hadn't moved from his spot.

"There was nothing I could do to stop it. I'm truly sorry Ines."

"Stop saying that!" It was then I noticed my whole body was shaking. Bile rose in my throat. I flew out of the living room and barely made it to the bathroom before I lost the meager contents of my stomach. My hair was pulled back and a cold cloth was pressed against the back of my neck. I lost track of how many times I retched. When there was nothing left in my stomach, I collapsed on the floor exhausted.

Strong arms lifted me off the ground. I was so heartsick I didn't even protest. What Tomás said couldn't be true. He had to be lying. Ernesto couldn't be dead. I was laid on my bed and that's when a sob escaped. A warm body cocooned my cold, shivering one as I released tortured cry after tortured cry. Time stopped moving. I felt utterly and completely dead inside. I wanted to die, too. Whispered words were spoken in my ear, but I was deaf to them. The voice continued to speak to me, and eventually my body quieted.

I was numb.

I heard one final whispered word in my ear before I knew nothing more.

"Sleep."

I STRUGGLED TO OPEN MY EYES. THEY FELT SO HEAVY. MY head was foggy and my mouth tasted like a sewer. I sluggishly sat up and wondered why I was in bed this early in the day. Then the memories rushed in. Ernesto. Oh, god. I fisted my mouth to hold back a scream.

A noise from the other room snapped me to attention, and the smell of coffee hit my nose.

Knowing who was out there and dreading seeing him, I pulled myself out of bed and delayed the meeting. Shuffling feet led me to the bathroom, where I brushed my teeth. After finishing, I stared at my reflection. Mascara was smeared under my eyes, which were red and bloodshot. My hair was tangled in some places and sticking up in others. A half sob escaped me that I even noticed that stupid stuff. My brother was dead and inconsequential bullshit like my hair or makeup didn't even fucking matter. The only thing that mattered was making sure the men who were responsible for Ernesto's death paid for what they'd done.

I grabbed a washcloth and cleaned my face. I combed the tangles out of my hair until it shined. Quickly changing my clothes, I took one final look at myself in the mirror before heading out to meet my nemesis. Tomás looked up when I entered the room. I hated that my body hummed when it spotted him. *Traitor.*

I forced myself to pay attention, because I realized he was speaking. "—if you wanted it. I wasn't sure how you took it."

Ah, yes, coffee. "Cream, no sugar."

When I moved to grab a mug, he waved me off. "Let me."

I changed course and sat at the dining room table I'd picked up at a garage sale a couple years ago. I'd stripped, sanded, and varnished it all on my own. It was the first time I'd done something like that, and I'd been proud of how well it turned out. Even Ernesto had been impressed.

Tomás stepped over to where I sat with a steaming mug in his hand and set it in front of me. I wrapped my hands around the mug and took several sips before staring at its contents like the answers I sought were inside.

"How long have you been a cop?" Tomás' voice came from across the table, and I realized he'd taken a seat while I'd savored my caffeine.

It was all part of my plan to answer his questions. "Five years."

He smiled. "I bet your brother loved that."

The ache in my heart grew, but I pushed it back. I needed to harden the damn organ if I was going to survive this.

"Not at first. Like any brother, he worried. Not about me not being able to handle the job, but that the job would change me. Seeing more bad than good messes with your psyche. But he had it all wrong. I saw more good than bad. And I thrived. Once he realized that, he'd never been prouder." I cleared my clogged throat.

"I assume that's why you were working the club. To get close to Alejandro to get information on where your brother might be."

It wasn't a question, but I answered anyway. "Yes."

"So, now what?"

I shrugged. "First, you answer my questions. Then, you go home and forget we ever had this conversation. Unless you plan on telling Miguel my real identity. If you haven't already. Then you'd have another death on your conscience. Or maybe you don't care."

Tomás jumped up so quickly his chair fell backward from the force. "Of course I fucking care, Ines. Do you really think I want to see you dead? Am I that much of a monster to you?"

I blinked at his outburst. I'd expected a reaction, but not this. This was fierce and fervent. I almost felt guilty. Almost. I still needed answers.

I choked out my response. "I'm sorry."

Tomás studied me, gauging my sincerity, before sighing. He picked his chair up off the floor and resumed sitting.

"I'll try to answer your questions. After that, I think the best thing you can do is go home and mourn with your family. Then, go back to work, and forget all about Miguel Álvarez."

It was painfully clear this man knew nothing about me. Otherwise, he'd know what he'd just said was ludicrous. There wasn't a chance in hell I'd ever forget.

"Who was it?" I asked, quickly changing gears.

Tomás brow crinkled. "Who was what?"

"Who pulled the trigger?" I demanded too quietly.

He shook his head. "It doesn't matter."

I slammed my fist on the table, rattling my mug. "Who killed my brother?"

CHAPTER 12

WHEN INES HAD ENTERED the kitchen, my heart skipped. Gone was all the glam. In place of the bombshell was a fresh-faced, naturally stunning woman. Ines looked several years younger than the twenty-six I knew her to be. She appeared untouched by the violent nature of our career choices. I, on the other hand, felt far older than thirty-eight.

Ignoring her question, I calmly refilled her mug.

Still lurking in the shadows of her eyes was grief, but a more powerful emotion was at the forefront. A quiet but ferocious storm was brewing. Which was perfectly fine with me. I'd much rather see violent fury than heart-crushing mourning. It only showcased how strong Ines was. My heart had broken at her cries, because I'd done that to her. Me. If only I'd tried harder to save her brother, she wouldn't have experience that level of pain and anguish. This was all my fault, and I would live with Ernesto Rodriguez's death on my shoulders for the rest of my life. I'd desperately wanted to tell her I was D.E.A., but there was no way I could. It was important, now more than ever, that she not find out. I was in too deep. I needed to protect her. One thing I did know, Paulo was a dead man. I was going to kill him for her.

"Someone who will die soon." There was a promise in my tone when I finally answered her.

Ines sensed it. "Why?"

I reached out and palmed the back of her neck. Her hair felt like silk beneath my fingers. Our foreheads touched as I leaned across the table, and her eyes darkened when I dropped a light kiss on her barely parted lips.

"Because what he did caused you pain. For that, he'll die."

AT ONE IN THE MORNING, I PULLED UP TO THE ABANDONED farmhouse and cut the lights of the light blue Chevy Impala almost as old as me. I kept it parked in a rented storage unit and only got it out when I didn't want to be seen. I exited the vehicle and popped the trunk. Surveying the contents of the lock box inside, I grabbed two sheathed knives and stuck one inside my left boot and the other I snapped onto my belt. Then, I palmed a small .22 and stuck it down my pants at the small of my back.

Then I took off at a slow clip, hopping a fence, and trekking through the dense copse of trees. I traveled three miles before the trees thinned and opened up to the back of a small, dark house. I kept in the shadows as I crept across the lawn before finally reaching the house. Using the knife at my back, I jimmied the window lock until it popped with a slight audible click. I stopped breathing, listening for any sounds of life inside the house. After five minutes with no alarm sounding, I slid the window open and crawled in.

My eyes slowly adjusted to the darkness, and I could make out an empty bed. I navigated the room, then down the hall to my intended destination. I could make out the shape of my target. I pulled out the gun and pressed it against temple of the sleeping man.

"I recommend you don't move. This thing might accidentally go off. We don't want that to happen. Yet."

A groggy Paulo responded. "What the fuck Tomás?"

"We have a problem, you and I."

He shifted and then winced when the barrel dug deeper into his skin. "I wouldn't recommend doing that again."

"What do you want?"

"You fucked up when you killed the cop, Paulo."

He sneered up at me. "*A la mierda con ese maldito puerco.*"

Rage had me seeing red. Before Paulo could even blink, I'd unsheathed the knife at my hip and sliced his throat. His hands went to his neck to stop the flow of blood that gurgled out. I leaned down and whispered in his ear. "The man you call a piece of shit pig was the brother of someone important to me. This is for her."

His eyes widened at that. I placed a pillow over his face and nestled the barrel of the gun deep into it before pulling the trigger twice, the stuffing muffling the sound. I exited the house as quietly as I'd arrived. I sprinted through the trees, and twenty minutes later I was back at the farmhouse, winded and sweating despite the cool morning air.

An hour later, I was inside yet another darkened house. This time, though, not to harm. Unable to help myself, I brushed the few strands of hair off Ines' sleeping face. She sighed softly, but otherwise didn't stir. Even when I leaned down to ghost my lips across her forehead. The crinkled note lay on the pillow next to her where she'd see it when she woke. I took one more longing glance at her face before disappearing into the waning moonlight.

CHAPTER 13

Sunlight filtering through my windows woke me, but I wasn't ready to get up yet and face the day. Today was my brother's funeral, and I couldn't be with my family to support them in case someone from the cartel was watching the service. It was killing me.

I forced myself out of bed anyway. Knowing my father would be worried sick, but needing to do this, I pulled the black netted hat out of its box and began to get ready. Two hours later, I was in my crappy jalopy driving down the road. I pulled into Zion Gardens Cemetery, exited my car, and started walking, my black heels occasionally sinking into the soft ground. I rounded a bend and stopped next to an old maple tree where I stood in its shadows. The netting from my hat was pulled down to cover my face, and, despite the heat, I wore a long-sleeved dress buttoned to the neck. I stood frozen like a statue as I watched the hearse crest a hill in the distance.

Memories of the last week came barreling back and I gasped at the pain. I let the tears fall. My brother was dead.

Immediately on its heels was Tomás' decree that he planned on killing my brother's murderer. The morning after I'd woken to find a piece of paper on my pillow. I'd opened the note to find a single sentence written in bold, slashing cursive. *It's done.* Below that, the letter T. I'd lain there for what seemed like hours, my feelings volleying between guilt and hope. A week later, I still hadn't figured out which emotion won out.

My eyes returned to the scene across the way and the scene in front of me blurred. The pallbearers, three of whom were my other brothers, had placed the casket on the lowering device. My eyes were dry and gritty, and I felt like I was suffocating. Warm fingers threaded through mine, and I knew without a doubt who stood next to me. Suddenly, I could breathe. I squeezed tightly, my fingernails digging into the back of Tomás' hand, and his gruff voice sounded in my ear.

"Stay strong, *raya*. For Ernesto."

"Did you mean what you said in your note?" My voice came out choked, my throat thick.

"Yes."

I swallowed down the thickness. "Thank you."

It seemed such an odd thing to say to someone who just confessed to murdering someone to avenge your family. He didn't respond. Only offered me his strength with a slight squeeze of his long, calloused fingers. We continued standing in silence as my brother was lowered into the ground. Tomás and I remained connected long after the grave had been covered and everyone dispersed, the sounds of our breathing the only noise between us. The sun was setting, but I didn't want to be alone. I turned toward him, my vision distorted by the netting covering my face.

"Why did you come?" I didn't understand this man. He was brutal, yet tender. My head kept screaming he was a criminal, while my heart kept seeing the man who'd held me in my grief. Both last week and again today.

He brought our threaded fingers to his mouth and kissed my knuckles, his eyes darkening with emotion. "Because you needed me."

I licked my dry lips, drawing his gaze downward, and his eyes darkened even further, this time with another emotion. My nipples pebbled beneath my dress.

Tomás broke the connection between us. "Come, it's getting late."

He pulled me away from our hiding spot and led me to my car. I finally noticed his motorcycle. I couldn't believe I hadn't heard his arrival.

"I'll follow you home. Make sure you get there safely." He opened the driver's side door for me.

I merely nodded before sliding behind the wheel and lifting the net from in front of my face.

Putting the car in drive, we exited the cemetery. I kept glancing in my review mirror while I drove home. He stayed right behind me the whole way. When I reached my front door, I stopped when his footfalls grew louder behind me. It was a sharp contrast between Tomás and Alejandro, who never once saw me inside. Inhaling for courage, I turned.

"Will you stay with me tonight? I don't think I can be alone." My words were barely above a whisper.

Tomás' look was pained. He shook his head. "It's not a good idea, Ines."

I clasped his hand between mine and squeezed it against my chest. "Please."

He warred with indecision, but I knew the moment he made his choice. He took the keys from my hand and led me inside, closing and locking the door behind us. I flipped on the light and removed my hat, laying it on the side table. Next I slipped out of my heels, leaving them at the door. I padded barefoot across the living room until I reached the kitchen, my body humming with awareness of the man following behind me. Tension radiated off him and I could hear his soft footsteps. I grabbed two beers out of the fridge and popped the top off both before turning and handing him one.

Our eyes connected and neither of us broke the contact. Tomás continued his white-knuckled hold on his at the same time I took a long pull from mine. My body thrummed and my core pulsed. A spark lit my fingers when he slipped the bottle from them, our skin grazing, and set both mine and his on the counter. In one long stride, he was almost pressed up against me. We were so close, we practically breathed in each other's air. My nipples hardened with arousal, and when he reached up and brushed a strand of hair off my face, tucking it behind my ear, my breath hitched.

"You're so beautiful and far too good for me." Tomás' voice was husky.

Slowly, he backed me up until I ran up against the counter, out of room, his arms caging my body. Not that I wanted to go anywhere. With infinite care, like he was waiting for me to stop him, Tomás dipped his head, our gazes still colliding, and brushed a kiss across my lips. His touch was featherlight, and I wanted more. I tried to deepen the kiss, but he wasn't having it. He pulled back, my body immediately missing his warmth.

"Come." He didn't bother asking. Instead, he reached for my hand and guided me to my bedroom.

When we reached the bed, I expected him to lay down and bring me with him. Instead, he issued another command.

"Sit here."

Again, I responded automatically and sat on the edge of the bed while he disappeared into the bathroom. Running water sounded and soon the smell of jasmine wafted out to tickle my nose. Steam soon followed. The water shut off and Tomás exited the bathroom. His palm found the back of my head and he lightly fisted my hair, pulling gently to tilt my head up so our eyes met.

"Your bath is ready. I want you to soak and relax. When you're finished, put on the robe hanging behind the door."

His lips dusted my forehead, and then I was alone in my room, my whole body tense with arousal. I squeezed my legs together to stop the throbbing. I quickly disrobed and headed to my bath.

CHAPTER 14

I SHOULDN'T BE HERE, but I'd been helpless to resist her broken plea. While Ines was in the bath, I paced. I tried not to imagine the water gliding across her caramel colored skin. I fought the images but they wouldn't stop flashing in my head. Soapy hands running up and down her body. Brown nipples pebbled in the cool air. I groaned at the image and adjusted my aching cock.

I froze at the click of the bathroom door. Then she was in front of me, her sweat-dampened hair piled on top of her head, her tight body hidden beneath the robe.

"Lay on your stomach." I barely recognized my own voice with the guttural command.

Ines moved to unbelt her robe.

"No." She froze at the harsh directive. I softened my tone. "No, leave it."

I exhaled when she obeyed. Her head was turned toward me and she observed me with eyes that begged me to touch her. I didn't know how long I could resist. I removed my suit jacket and folded it over the back of her vanity seat before rolling my cuffs up to my elbows. Her gaze tracked my every move and her pupils widened. I toed off my shoes, but everything else remained on. I sat next to her and began to knead her shoulders, keeping my touch gentle. Her eyes grew heavy, and she moaned when I hit certain spots. I bit my lip to not respond with a groan of my own.

I moved down Ines' body, her warm skin now under mine as I massaged and kneaded her thighs and calves. She let out a long sigh of satisfaction when I reached her feet. Up and down I massaged, staying on top of her robe, even as it slid up to expose the crease of her thigh under her ass cheek. Her breathing grew shallow, and I knew she was almost asleep. The day had taken its toll. When I thought she was asleep, I slipped the sheet over her.

I shrugged back into my jacket and donned my shoes. I'd almost made my escape when her sleepy voice had me pausing in my tracks.

"You said you'd stay."

I turned back. She was on her side, elbow crooked, her head resting on her open palm, that damn robe gaping open and offering me a glimpse of her rounded breast. Her drowsy, sex-kitten eyes beckoned me.

"It's not a good idea, Ines," I repeated my earlier words.

"Just hold me until I fall asleep. Please."

This woman slayed me. Knowing I'd regret my decision, I once again found myself jacket-less and shoe-less. Only now I was on my back, in a bed belonging to a woman I couldn't have, holding her luscious body against my side, her arm across my chest.

~

WARM, WET HEAT CLOSED AROUND MY COCK, AND A TONGUE circled the bulbous tip at the same time a hand squeezed the base with just the right amount of pressure. I fisted her hair and pulled the woman's head down at the same time I thrust upward. Coughing ensued when I hit the back of her throat and she pulled away, startling me awake. The fog receded and I realized I wasn't dreaming.

"Ines," I groaned when she returned to her task.

"Let me." She stared up at me with pleading eyes.

Pleasure overrode common sense. Once again her head lowered and my cock disappeared inside her mouth. Up and down she moved, taking me further with each downward motion until I reached the back of her throat again. Her hands gently squeezed and cupped my balls, rolling them between her fingers. My fingers threaded through her hair and my pelvis moved of its own accord, gently thrusting upward to meet her.

"Relax your throat."

On command, Ines responded and she took me even deeper. My balls tightened, and I could feel my climax building.

"I'm going to come," I warned even though I didn't slow my thrusts. In response, she only took a deep breath and completely relaxed her throat, engulfing my entire cock, never once taking her eyes off me. The move was so fucking hot, I couldn't stop my release, and she swallowed everything I gave her. Once I'd emptied myself, she pulled away, saliva and come running out the side of her mouth. God, that was so fucking sexy. Her eyes widened when I traced the moisture with my thumb and licked it off.

The sexual haze began to clear and I knew that this was

only the beginning. Despite my earlier conviction, I couldn't let Ines go. It wasn't the near-perfect blow job that changed my mind either. Ines was more stubborn than me. It was time to acknowledge the truth I'd been fighting for far too long. She was mine, and I planned on doing whatever I could to not only keep her, but protect her. With my life if necessary.

"Come here."

She scooted upward and I wrapped my arm around her, pulling her close to me.

"What were you like as a girl?"

I couldn't see it, but I could almost feel her smile. "I was a hellion. Had no real idea how to be a little girl. I pestered my brothers to no end. Ernesto was the one I drove the most crazy. He was almost ten years older than me. He once told me he started going gray at fifteen because of me. Victor is the nearest in age to me, so I was always closest to him growing up. There were no such things as boy stuff and girl stuff to me. Exploring the mountains near where we lived in Colorado was my most favorite thing to do."

I could picture her as a young girl, hair braided while she trekked up and down the mountains, not caring if she got dirty or scraped her knees. "I'm sure you kept your brothers on their toes."

She giggled, the sound carefree. "Of course. I couldn't let them think they were better than me. It was important their heads didn't get too big."

The sun had long risen, and I knew it was time to get up, but I was reluctant to leave her arms. Except, we needed to talk.

CHAPTER 15

AFTER TOMÁS LEFT THE ROOM, I flopped back on the bed, my body still humming. When I'd woken in his arms, I studied him. I didn't know his actual age, but based on the few strands of gray hair I noticed at his temples and the lines near his eyes, I put him in his late-thirties. In sleep, he looked younger.

I didn't know what was going to happen between us. Over the last week, I'd been pulling further and further away from Alejandro. There was no need to entice him for information about my brother anymore. Ernesto was dead.

After I'd recovered from the news of his death, I'd had the bright idea of seducing Tomás for cartel information, but an inner voice had stopped that train of thought. Regardless of us being on opposite sides of the law, there was something about him that spoke to me. Like I recognized some inherent good in him, despite who his employer was.

I jumped out of the bed, washed my face, and slipped into a comfortable pink t-shirt and white shorts. I'd foregone shoes, which made my feet enter the living room soundlessly. I stood in the doorway for a few minutes absorbing the sight of him. He'd put his shoes back on, and his jacket was firmly buttoned and covering his body like armor. I knew he wanted to put distance between us, and his attire helped. Oddly though, he looked like he belonged here in this house. Even though I knew it was a ridiculous daydream, I envisioned him being here when I got home from a hard day at the precinct, greeting me with a kiss. I shook off the thought, because it was insanity. We should be, were, enemies, yet I couldn't think of him that way.

Sensing my presence, he finally lifted his head. Our eyes connected, and I read so many different emotions. Lust, regret, guilt. I stepped fully into the room and sat on the couch, my leg tucked underneath me.

"How did you know where to find me?"

"I knew when the funeral was, and I just thought you might need some support."

Tomás' words shocked and confused me. "What if they had been watching? You work for Miguel, Tomás. I'm a cop even if you're the only one who knows. How were you going to explain either of us being there? Especially...together."

That's what they'd assume. That he and I were together. That I was cheating on Alejandro. Tomás merely shrugged like it was of no consequence.

"They weren't."

"Alejandro would kill you if he thought I was cheating on him. It doesn't matter that I've practically broken up with him."

"I can handle Alejandro." Tomás' confidence was apparent. "Don't worry Ines. I'll protect you."

I jumped up from the couch, my fists clenched at my sides. "But who's going to protect *you*?"

In two strides, he was in front of my cupping my cheeks in his large hands, staring intensely down at me. "Don't worry about me. I can protect myself, I promise."

"I never slept with Alejandro. Not even to get information about my brother."

His smile was cocky. "I know."

"You don't know that."

His smile never dimmed.

"You don't," I insisted mulishly.

"*Raya*, there isn't a chance in hell you slept with that punk." I found his confidence extremely sexy. Irritating, but sexy.

"And how do you know that?"

Now, his smile flattened and a darkness flared in his eyes. "Because if you'd slept with Alejandro, I'd have to kill him."

Oh. The bloodthirsty statement shouldn't have me hot and bothered, but holy hell. There must be something seriously wrong with me. "I guess that means I'm breaking up with him." I joked uncomfortably.

Tomás didn't smile. "I guess so."

Apparently today was the day for confessions, because I couldn't stop another one from spilling from my lips. "I'd planned on seducing you for cartel business information."

This time, a small smile graced his lips. "Is that what this morning was all about?"

Surprisingly, I blushed. "No. This morning was purely for want and desire. It shouldn't have happened though."

"No, it shouldn't have."

My voice dropped. "It's going to happen again though, isn't it?"

Tomás stepped back into my personal space, reached out for the end of my braid, and wrapped it around his fist, gently pulling me forward. He lowered his head, but stopped just before his lips reached mine. His breath tickled and I unconsciously licked my lips, my tongue inadvertently flicking against his mouth. He drew in a sharp breath.

"Most definitely. And more."

My entire body shivered at the promise in his tone.

CHAPTER 16

I KNEW I should regret what happened between Ines and me, but I couldn't. She'd become an addiction I didn't want to kick. She'd been taken aback when I said I'd have to kill Alejandro. It wasn't a lie. Jealous rage boiled my blood thinking of that little shit touching her. For the first time in five years, I was rethinking my undercover work. Yes, I'd proven my skills over the years by leading the D.E.A. to bust hundreds, if not thousands of drug deals. We'd slowed Miguel for a while, but it always seemed like for every dealer within the organization we brought down, two more would pop up.

For so long, my obsession with stopping the sale of drugs had been my life goal. Now, though, I'd promised I would protect Ines, which meant I needed to stay away, but that proved impossible if the last two days were any indication. Before I'd left her house yesterday, I'd programmed her number into my phone with a promise to call her.

In the meantime, I was on my way to a meeting with Miguel to discuss the latest deal. It was guaranteed to be a lucrative one with a lot of drugs and a lot of money exchanging hands. It was also a deal the D.E.A. would be busting.

Son of a bitch.

I spotted a familiar silver Porsche. Reluctantly, I'd driven my "office car", instead of my Softail. The Audi R8 Spyder was far more conducive to conducting drug deals than a Harley. Miguel had paid for the car, and it was definitely a beaut, but it made me feel claustrophobic. I needed the rush of air and the open space that came from my bike.

I wandered through each room, the soles of my shoes clicking on the marble floor and echoing throughout the high-ceilings, before exiting the French doors and heading out into the courtyard. The temperature was about fifteen degrees warmer than the air conditioned inside of the house, but about ten degrees cooler than if the whole area wasn't entirely shaded by the giant trees spread throughout.

Miguel and Alejandro were seated at a table near the pool, each sipping, based on the snifter housing it, Miguel's favorite liquor from Mexico, Sotol. Approaching the duo, I pasted on a smile.

"Greetings, Miguel. Alejandro."

Miguel rose with hand outstretched. "Ah, Tomás, so good to see you. Would you like a drink?"

I shook my head. "No, thank you, though. I prefer a clear head when discussing business. So, what's the plan for tomorrow?"

"Always focused on work, aren't you, *mi amigo*?" He laughed like he'd made a joke.

"Oh, I think there are other things our *friend* here

focuses on." Alejandro interjected with a hint of dark sarcasm.

I studied him briefly. His pose was deceivingly relaxed. I didn't glance in Miguel's direction, but I wondered if he spotted it as well. Deciding it was always best to go on the offensive to throw people off, I volleyed back my own question. "Are you inferring something? If so, why don't you just say it instead of throwing out vague comments?"

He sputtered and cast several glances at his uncle, who smirked. Despite his charm and debonair persona, Miguel was a ruthless, power- and money-hungry drug lord. Familial emotions aside, I truly believed he'd see Alejandro dead and a new leader chosen before he let anyone destroy the business he'd built.

Alejandro must have grown a set, because he snapped his shirt sleeves taut, straightened in his chair, and sent me a glaring look over the top of his nose.

"You've been absent an awful lot lately, and Gabby has been avoiding me. I'm not stupid."

That's debatable. Knowing that wouldn't go over well, I offered instead, "You're kidding me. There are more important things you should be focusing on than some whore who decides she's not interested anymore. Your uncle is trying to teach you how to run this business, and you're thinking with your cock instead of your brain."

Calling Ines a whore stuck in my throat, but it was the only thing to say. Alejandro's neck and face flushed red, and his whole body went rigid at my insult. His eyes shone with an intense, fevered hatred. My face was slack with boredom. I'd learned a lot about Miguel Álvarez over the last five years, and I knew he wouldn't intervene. He'd want to see how his nephew handled the situation.

I was actually shocked when Alejandro reined in his hatred. A calm façade slid over him, before he gave me a conciliatory smile. "You're right. She is worthless, nothing but *una puta*, and doesn't deserve my attention. *La familia* is most important."

A tense silent reigned between us, until finally Miguel broke it. "Now that we have that settled, it's time to get down to business. Alejandro, you will go with Tomás next month. He will introduce you to our supplier so he can become familiar with you. You will take his lead. This deal is important. I plan on cultivating a relationship with Raúl Escobar to rival that of the Sinaloa Cartel if I have plans of taking over their supply line."

It felt like a test. One I didn't want to fail. When there was no disagreement or pushback, my instincts roared out a warning signal. Listening to it had saved my life more than once. Looked like I planned on keeping a closer eye on junior. *Fuck.*

CHAPTER 17

I'D THOUGHT of nothing but Tomás since he left this morning, and I desperately needed Estelle's advice. Knowing it wasn't the smartest idea, I called her anyway.

"Hello."

"Hey, Bubbles." I used Estelle's childhood nickname so she knew it wasn't safe to talk over the phone.

"You're hilarious. You know I outgrew that name years ago." She sounded appropriately aggrieved, although I knew for a fact that the nickname didn't bother her at all. She still laughed about it, except when Victor used it. Now, *that* irritated her.

"I know, but it's still fun to harass you with it."

"Yeah, yeah. So, how's it going?"

"Good. I was calling to see if you were free for lunch?"

"Yeah, absolutely. When and where?"

I thought about it for a minute. "How about one, at my favorite sushi place?"

"That sounds perfect actually. I've been craving sushi for days."

"Great, I'll see you then."

After hanging up, I hopped in the shower. While I was getting ready, I thought about what I was going to tell Estelle. I wanted to keep Tomás to myself for a bit. I was honest enough to know that it was in part due to the fact that I was a little ashamed at my feelings. He was so bad for me for so many reasons, but I couldn't seem to control myself now that I'd had a taste of him. I wanted to blame it on high emotions, especially after Ernesto's death, or raging hormones, but that wasn't entirely it. There was this essence about him that called to me. It wasn't rational, but it was there. Still not sure what I was going to say, I headed to the restaurant.

I arrived at Roka Akor ten minutes early. Not that I had any reason to believe someone would follow me, but I was still being cautious. I sat at our regular table near the bar and waited for Estelle to arrive. Forever on time, she walked through the door at exactly one p.m.. I rose and gave her a hug before we both took our seats.

"So," she drew the word out, "what's going on? Is everything okay?"

"It's safe to talk here," I assured her.

Estelle looked relieved that she didn't need to act. She reached out to clutch my hand. "Oh my god, Ines, I'm so sorry about Ernesto. I know you well enough to hear the strain in your voice when you called. You certainly didn't sound like you were good. It broke my heart when I heard the news, and I couldn't be there for you. I hate that you weren't at the funeral."

"Actually, I was," I blurted out. "God, Estelle, I'm in so much trouble."

Her eyes widened in horror. "Shit, do they know?"

I knew what she was asking. "No. Well, Tomás knows."

I didn't think her eyes could get any bigger, but I was wrong. "Holy fuck. Do you mean the same Tomás from the club that night? How did he find out? Oh my god, Ines, you need to tell Victor."

"He won't say anything."

"How do you know? Ines, he's a member of the fucking cartel, and he knows you're a cop who is—was—dating his boss' nephew. From the brief conversation we had, Tomás doesn't strike me as dumb. He has to know there was a reason you would be dating Alejandro. And not because you were in love with him. You're going to get yourself killed."

Her voice rose with the last, and I shushed her when I spotted the waiter approaching. She blurted out her order to get him moving along. When he left, I spoke again.

"Estelle, you have to trust me. He's not going to tell anyone."

She stared at me for the longest time, until her expression shifted to one of disbelief. "Jesus, Mary, and Joseph. You have a thing for him. This is bad. Like really, really bad. You know that, right?"

"It gets worse."

Her eyes closed briefly, and I could almost see the mental prayer she was sending up. "Please, please don't tell me you slept with him."

"I didn't sleep with him."

"But..." This was why Estelle was my best friend. She knew me better than anyone.

"I was at the cemetery. He showed up, Estelle. Told me he didn't think I should be alone. Stayed with me the whole time. Held me throughout the night. When I woke in his arms this morning, I couldn't stop myself. It just sort of happened."

She rubbed her forehead like she was warding off a headache. "Oh, Ines."

"I know. I can't explain it. Tomás stands for everything I despise. I fight every day to bring down criminals. The same criminals who killed Ernesto. There's something different about him, Estelle. We're on entirely different sides of the law, but I'm blinded by an inherent goodness I swear I sense in him. Which makes absolutely no sense. I'm so confused, and I know that this, whatever it is, is going to end badly. Like so epically disastrous, but I don't know if I can stop it. I don't know that I want to."

She clasped my hands. "I just don't want to see you hurt. Something we both know is going to happen. This isn't going to end in a happily ever after, Ines. Any relationship between you is going to crash and burn. One of you isn't going to survive the fire. I'm terrified it's going to be you. Your family can't survive another loss. I couldn't survive. You're my best friend. I can't lose you."

I squeezed her hand hard. "You're not going to lose me, Estelle. I swear."

She looked at me sadly. "I hope you're right."

Our waiter arrived with our sushi, but I'd lost my appetite. We ate in relative silence, with me picking at my food. After we finished eating, we said our goodbyes and I headed home, more conflicted than ever. Everything she'd said was true. There would be no happy ending for Tomás and me. And still I was willing to take the risk. I was so fucked. I'd just closed my front door when my text alert sounded. My heart skipped a beat and then started racing when I saw Tomás' number and the message.

Garden of the Phoenix footbridge
7:00 p.m.

Torn with indecision, I quickly typed out a response and hit send before I could change my mind.

CHAPTER 18

SHORTLY AFTER SIX, I exited the 59th Street train station. Then, on foot, I headed east. I walked for close to fifteen minutes before finally reaching my destination. The Garden of the Phoenix is out in the middle of an island in Jackson Park near Chicago's Museum of Science and Industry on the south side of the city. It's so secluded that a majority of locals have never heard of it. Not my mother, though. It had been one of her favorite places to visit after the city had restored and redesigned it when I was a freshman in high school. I came here once a week in her memory. And unless you knew where you were going, it could be hard to find. It was also surrounded by a neighborhood of drugs and gang violence, which deterred a lot of visitors in the evening hours, making it the perfect meeting place.

I stood on the footbridge, forearms resting against the wood, and watched the setting sun, thinking of Ines and wondering what the hell I was going to do. I'd been schooled countless times during training to avoid personal entanglements while undercover. It was a surefire way to get myself killed. Number one rule of surviving was to become the person you'd created. It wasn't a mask you donned and doffed each day. Every aspect of your life revolved around who you now were. The line between right and wrong blurred. For five years, I'd done that. Except over the last two days, I'd stopped being Tomás González and had returned to being Brody Thomas. All because of a woman. Because of Ines.

Every instinct told me she'd be at the cemetery, which was why I'd followed her. I knew she was strong. But if there was one thing that could bring her to her knees, it was not being able to be with her family. She'd seemed so brittle, standing there alone, that she could break any moment. So, I offered her my strength. Because I wanted her to see me. *Brody.*

It wasn't long before I sensed Ines' presence. Her scent caught on the almost always-present Chicago breeze and mingled with the blooming cherry blossoms. She moved into my periphery and mirrored my pose. Silently, we stood looking out over the water, the cool night air kissing our skin, the sound of crickets and frogs our only companion.

"When I was almost ten, my mom found out she was pregnant. Her long-term boyfriend didn't believe her when she told him it was his, and he took off. At first, my mom was devastated. Then she was determined. Determined that she raise her sons to be good, strong men who took care of their women. When my brother was born, I was so envious of the attention he received. Until one day my mom had to run down to the laundry room and asked me to keep an eye on him while she was gone. She hadn't even been out of the apartment five minutes when Preston started screaming. I was terrified, and I started to panic. Not knowing what else to do, I stood over his crib and started singing to him. Like that, he stopped and just stared up at me and blinked, his eyes watery with unshed tears. It was in that moment that I fell in love with him. After that day, I sang to him whenever he was upset, and every time he'd stop crying. There were times I swear he'd start to cry just to hear me sing."

I smiled at the memory. I continued softly, my eyes remaining forward. "Anyway, I'm glad you came."

She remained quiet for a moment longer. "I almost didn't."

"What made you change your mind?"

I felt more than saw her shrug. "To be honest, I really don't know."

I turned toward her. She was absolutely breathtaking. The colors of the sunset glowed behind her, making her hair sparkle with shades of yellow, gold, and burnt orange. It fell down around her shoulders like the first day I'd met her. Then she'd worn a killer, sexy-as-fuck dress and heels that I pictured digging into my back while I rode her. Today, she was dressed casually in a curve hugging sweater that accentuated her small waist, a pair of jeans, and pink canvas shoes. Her makeup was minimal which made her look like your basic girl next door. Except there nothing basic about her.

Unable to stop myself, and not wanting to anyway, I took a step forward, brushing her hair off her neck and over her shoulder, its texture like silk against my skin. Her large, chocolate eyes stared up at me, pupils darkening with every breath we took, and her pink tongue darted out to wet her lips in anticipation. My nostrils flared at the gesture. I reached out with my free hand and rubbed my thumb over the wetness. Needing a taste of her like I needed my next breath, I cupped her cheek and lowered my head, my lips covering hers. Immediately she opened, letting me deepen the kiss. I swallowed her moan when her small fists clutched my biceps. It was my first true taste of her, and she tasted like the sweetest of berries.

Our first kiss had been about comfort. This one was filled with forbidden desire. When I'd sent that text and she responded, we both knew where this would lead. The kiss continued, each of us breathing the other in, while I reveled in her softness. Within this hidden paradise, there was only the two of us. The entire world outside the border of this tiny island didn't exist. Tomás and Gabriela didn't exist. In here, we were Brody and Ines.

I pulled back, needing to see her. She mewled in disappointment at the loss of contact. Our breathing was heavy in the night air as she blinked up at me with drowsy eyes, her lips puffy and well-kissed. My cock was rock-hard, but tonight, this first time between us, was about all about her. It might be our one and only time together, and I wanted to brand her with my touch. So that no matter what happened after tonight, she would remember me. I wanted to take her gently, then rough. I wanted her nails to score my back while she screamed out her orgasm.

"Come with me." My voice was deep and guttural with desire as I took her hand.

Silently, we retraced the path I'd taken to get here. "Are you sure you want to do this, Ines? Have you really thought about who I am? Who you are?"

Ines paused in reflection, and I waited for her to realize

what a mistake she was making. She was a dedicated police officer and, as far as she was concerned, I was a drug-dealing member of the Mexican cartel. We were not meant to be together, no matter how deep the attraction ran.

She turned her body toward me and squeezed my hand. "I don't know your story and why you do what you do. My whole life I thought that bad people were bad while good people were good. Until I joined the force. Over the last five years I've come to learn that there are good people who do bad things. There are also bad people who do good things."

She swallowed.

"Going into law enforcement, we know, on some level, there's a chance we can be killed in the line of duty. It's something we ignore and hope it goes away. But with Ernesto's death, I could no longer ignore it. I was devastated, but it also made me question my own mortality. I knew how hard it was for you to tell me about my brother. I could see it. As crazy as it seems, I think you're one of those good people who does bad things. You were there for me during one of the hardest moments of my life. I know this… affair, I guess, between us won't last. It can't. Not with us on opposite sides of the law. But, for a brief time, I want to do what I do when it comes to thinking about death. I'm going to ignore it and hope it goes away."

She'd made her decision.

I was done resisting. The only thing I could do now was to protect her as best I could from any fallout.

We walked the remaining few blocks to my flat. I flipped the light to illuminate the living room. It was then I realized what I'd done. I'd brought Ines to my place. *Brody's* place. Shit.

CHAPTER 19

"Would you like something to drink?"

"I'll take some water if you don't mind."

"Not at all. Why don't you make yourself at home? I'll be right back."

While Tomás was gone, I wandered the room, pausing at the mantle where several family photos were displayed.

"Here you go."

I startled a little, like I'd been caught snooping. I couldn't hold back my curiosity though.

"Is that your mom and brother? You boys resemble each other." I gestured with the bottle he'd handed me.

"Yes."

I blinked at his succinct, one-word answer. Apparently there weren't supposed to be any personal questions. Considering who we were, I guess that was understandable. I sipped my water to swallow back my hurt at his abruptness.

"Sorry, that was rude." He shifted uncomfortably like apologies weren't something he made often.

"No, no, I get it. I shouldn't have asked."

Tomás stepped into my space, forcing me to look up at him at the same time my body heated at his closeness. I could smell his cologne, he stood so close. "It's a perfectly reasonable observation to make and question to ask. It wasn't off-limits. Just a painful topic."

"I'm sorry." And I was. It hadn't been my intent to cause him pain. I couldn't help my naturally inquisitive nature.

"Don't be."

When he stepped away, I was bereft at the loss of his scent and warmth. He'd smelled so good, I'd wanted to bury my nose against his neck and breathe him in. His gaze focused on the picture behind me.

"My mother died ten years ago. A kid, high on heroin, tried to steal her purse from her. When she didn't give it up, he pushed her. She fell and hit her head so hard, it ruptured an aneurysm in her brain. She died instantly."

I covered my mouth with my hand to hold back my horrified gasp. "Tomás, I'm so sorry. I can't imagine how awful that was for you."

He gave a self-deprecating laugh. "That's not the worst of it. My brother was the doped-up kid who killed her."

He stood rigidly next to me, and I wrapped my arms around his waist and laid my head against his chest. For several heartbeats he continued to remain stiff, but eventually his muscles relaxed and he retuned my embrace. We stood there for the longest time, simply a man and woman finding and receiving strength from the other. Soon, though, my thoughts shifted to how warm and hard he felt beneath me.

Slowly, I tilted my head up. Tomás' eyes were heated.

Standing on tiptoe, I reached up to brush my lips across his. His hands shifted slightly downward until he gripped my hips, pulling me ever so closer until his erection pressed against my stomach. That was all it took to set me off. My hands traveled upward and my fingers fisted in his hair to pull his head down to meet mine and I deepened the kiss.

Typically, I didn't like to lead when it came to the bedroom, but I think it put Tomás' mind at ease that this was really what I wanted. Being in control here also made me feel powerful. I could bring this man to his knees.

Hands roamed, both sets. Lips and tongues met, breaths mingled. Moans and gasps filled the air. I didn't know where I ended and Tomás began. For this moment, we were like one, our bodies so close. My nose filled with the scent of his cologne and his own manly scent, and it was intoxicating. I was drunk on his smell, his taste.

"Bedroom?" I gasped against his lips, and felt an answering smile.

"Eager, are we?"

I nipped at his bottom lip then soothed it with my tongue. "You have no idea. I fought against it, but I've wanted to see you naked and begging for me since that first day out by Miguel's pool. I spotted you the minute you entered the courtyard, and couldn't take my eyes off you while you practically prowled across the brick sidewalk. You exuded danger, and although I desperately lusted after you, I knew I had to avoid you because of who I was."

His grin was oh so cocky. "'Desperately lusted after', huh? What makes you think I'll be the one begging?"

"Wanna place a bet?" My answering smile was cheeky.

"I don't ever bet if I know I'm going to lose." He winked at me.

Wow, this charming side of Tomás was making me weak in the knees. And we were only getting started.

"Is that why you've yet to lead us in the direction of the bedroom?"

His hand left my hip and wrapped around mine. "I won't let it be said that I kept a woman waiting."

He led me down the darkened hallway, my eyes slow to adjust to the unfamiliar surroundings, until we reached the last room at the end. When he flipped the lights on, I blinked at the brightness and then scanned the room, hoping to get a glimpse into the personality of this intriguing man. If I thought seeing his bedroom, his personal sanctum, would clue me in, I was sadly mistaken. The whole room was utilitarian. The walls were painted white with no pictures or decorations displayed. There was a large bed against the opposite side of the room, its comforter a plain, basic navy. Next to the bed was a night-stand made of dark wood, a single lamp with plain white shade standing on it. Also gracing the top of the stand was a cheap black alarm clock, its lights blinking the incorrect time, like no one had cared to change it after a power outage.

There was a matching dresser on the nearest wall to where we entered, a layer of dust across the top. It was next to a closed door which I assumed was a closet and on the third wall was an open door, the reflection of the room bouncing off the mirror I could just spy. There was also a smell of disuse in the air. Like no one had lived here for a while. There weren't any stray clothes strewn anywhere. It was neat and tidy, if slightly dusty, and had an unused feel. It was a puzzle I pushed to the back of my mind. Sure, it was reckless of me, but I ignored the feeling. Especially when Tomás drew me in his arms.

"Are you ready to make me beg now?"

CHAPTER 20

WITH TOMÁS' question, my body ignited. Power rushed through me. In response to his question, I sent him a look of pure seduction. Feeling bold, I reached down and pulled my sweater up and over my head before tossing it to the floor. His eyes smoldered with heat and followed my movements as I reached behind my back, unhooking my bra. Teasingly, I dragged the straps down one arm, then the other, before dropping it to land on the floor next to my shirt. His fists clenched, like he resisted reaching out to touch me, perhaps afraid I would stop if he did, and his nostrils flared like he could scent my arousal, which only made me wetter. I toed off my shoes and kicked them to the side. Continuing my seductive tease, I unbuttoned my jeans, and slowly pushed them down my legs, kicking them off to land with the rest of my clothes. His breathing became ragged and his eyes darkened to almost pitch.

Now, I stood in only my teeny tiny thong. Our eyes met and stayed connected while I pushed the scrap of fabric down until gravity helped them slide to the floor. I stepped out of them while Tomás practically panted. Tossing off a wink, I pivoted, and with a little extra swing to my hips, I made my way to the bed. I settled myself on top of the covers, reclining back on my elbows and, with the crook of one finger, beckoned Tomás to join me.

I giggled when he frantically began ripping his own clothes off. When he realized what he was doing, he sent me a goofy smile and slowed down his movements until, finally, he was blessedly naked. My eyes drank in his now fully exposed body. I started at the top and my eyes followed the lines of his broad shoulders down to his tapered waist. I counted each and every one of his abs. My mouth watered at that sexy V of his hips that always seemed to strike women stupid. Finally, my gaze zeroed in on his cock, and I gulped down the saliva gathering in my mouth. He was long and almost too thick. I didn't remember him being this big.

I'd been with only a few men in my life, and none of them compared to the gorgeous, and slightly intimidating, specimen before my eyes. My pussy throbbed with the knowledge that although I knew it would fit, there would definitely be the sting of the hurts-so-good kind. I could hardly wait.

I couldn't take my eyes off his cock as Tomás strode toward me. He placed his knee on the bed and hoisted himself up so he was on all fours above me. I looked up at him and lost myself in his gaze. I'd never felt this connection with someone before. He lowered himself until almost every part of our bodies were touching. Automatically, my legs separated to make room for him.

Tomás body was like a furnace. He was hot and hard and I couldn't help but rock my hips a little to create friction. I gasped as sparks ignited between us. He caged my head with his forearms, keeping his full weight off me, and when he slammed his mouth down on mine I clutched him tight, trying to anchor myself. He fisted my hair, the small pinch of pain causing me to gasp and to my surprise, I felt my pussy gush with wetness at the sensation. I never would have guessed I liked a little pain with my pleasure, but my body was basking in it. Tomás deepened the kiss and devoured my lips like he would never get enough of their taste. Tongues tangled, teeth gnashed, and I was gasping for breath when he pulled back to stare down at me. Our eyes met, and I saw his had darkened to almost black with arousal. I realized he was breathing just as heavy as me.

"You're fucking beautiful, Ines. I want this memory of you, right here, right now to stay with me forever. No matter what happens, I want to remember this night with you always. You are such a strong woman that any man would be lucky to call his."

Tomás' words almost sounded like a goodbye. It was something I didn't want to think about. I only wanted to feel.

"Kiss me again," I commanded, my fingers tangling in his hair and pulling him back down to me.

He immediately complied and more as his mouth nipped my bottom lip before ghosting along my jaw and into the sensitive crease in my neck. I tilted my head to give him better access. His tongue dampened my skin, and his breath warmed it. I should have guessed his intent, but I still gasped when hot moisture enveloped my breast. I couldn't help tighten my grip on his hair, which I quickly loosened when I felt him flinch against me.

"Sorry."

He released my nipple with a pop and tilted his head to smile up at me.

"A little hair pulling never hurt anyone." He winked before returning to his task.

Tomás paid homage to both breasts, with either his mouth or his hand while he plucked and tweaked my puckered tips. I giggled when he brushed his lips over my belly. His scruff tickled. He didn't stop his movements while he settled his broad shoulders between my parted thighs. His eyes darted up and our gazes met and held. I watched his fingers part my lower lips and then his tongue swiped a path up my slit taking my juice with it. My breath was coming in shallow gasps now, and I couldn't take my eyes away. Tomás licked his lips as if savoring my flavor. Then he lowered his head again. This time he didn't stop with a single lick. He nibbled and sucked and flicked his tongue, finding the perfect rhythm and pressure to drive me wild.

He shifted and hooked my knees over his shoulders before pulling me closer and opening me wider. I was helpless to do anything else, but let him continue his sensual assault. My bones were like jelly, and I was putty in his hands. When he speared my opening, pushing his tongue in deeper and deeper, my thighs actually quivered. Tomás was merciless while he sipped and drank down my juices. I was on the verge of orgasm and then, without warning, it struck and I had no choice in losing eye contact, because my head was thrown back in ecstasy. Tremors racked my body, and I cried out his name.

Small quakes still fluttered inside me, especially when he slid back up my body and stared down at me, his mouth glistening. It was so fucking sexy, and this weird need came over me. A need to see how we tasted together. I pulled Tomás' head down to me and plunged my tongue in his mouth, sampling our mixed flavors. It was erotic and sexy and we both tasted amazing. He groaned at my action and then pulled back, caging my head between his arms.

"Mmm, I love how we taste." I licked my lips, drawing in a blend of his natural mint flavor and my musky sweetness.

"God, that was so fucking hot."

"I don't know what came over me. It was a compulsion I couldn't resist."

"Well, feel free to do that anytime. And for the record, I love how *you* taste."

I ran my hands up and down his back, my body languid and relaxed after its orgasm. But my body needed more.

"Now that you've had your taste, I want more. There's an ache inside me."

"Where? Here?" Tomás' cock slid against my wet slit he'd just ravished and I could hear my desire. I pushed up against him and we both sighed when he butted up to my opening.

"God, yes. Please." My nails left indents in his back I clutched him so hard. He sat up a little, and I watched him reach into the nightstand and pull something out before shutting the drawer he'd retrieved it from. Then, I squeaked in surprise when Tomás suddenly rolled us and I was now on top. He held out the small square item.

"Put it on."

I gave him a cocky half-smile before plucking it from his fingers. With expertise, I ripped open the wrapper and rolled the condom down his cock. Tomás eyes glowed brightly as I concentrated on my task.

"Now, ride me."

"With pleasure."

I smiled with sexual satisfaction. Lifting my hip, I straddled him, rocking my pelvis against his creating an exquisite friction. Then, placing one hand on his chest, I braced myself while I raised up, reached back with my other hand to position his cock at my entrance. With Tomás' hands on my hips, guiding my descent, I slowly lowered myself down onto him. He clutched my hips tightly, no doubt leaving marks on my skin, when I stopped to breathe a couple times and get used to the sensation of him going deeper. I was right though. The burn of being stretched so wide hurt so good.

A moan of pleasure vibrated in my throat as his entire length finally filled me. Instinctively, I tightened my inner muscles, squeezing his cock tightly. Tomás' answering groan vibrated through my entire body, sending shockwaves through my pussy. I could feel his cock actually throbbing. I threw my head back, causing my breasts to thrust forward. I gasped when his large and calloused hands cupped them. I reached up and covered his hands with mine, squeezing them to provide the stimulus I was begging for.

"Fuck, you feel amazing inside me."

Tomás huffed out a laugh at my dirty talk. For some reason, I thought it had been a long time since he'd laughed. "It feels amazing to be inside you."

I looked down at him with a siren's smile, my hair a delicious mess dancing around my face and over my hand-covered breasts. Needing to feel Tomás' kiss, I swept it over one shoulder before leaning down and melding my mouth with his, a hint of my flavor still lingering on his lips. Then, I began to move.

CHAPTER 21

"Can I ask a personal question?"

I lay cuddled up next to Tomás, my arm thrown across his chest while I traced random patterns over his skin. He stiffened against me, but so quickly relaxed that I almost thought I imagined his tension. We'd been sleeping together for almost a week now, and I really didn't know anything about him. I thought once would be enough to get him out of my system and I'd no longer care. Except my thirst hadn't been nearly quenched. Neither my thirst for his body or my thirst for knowledge about him. He was a conundrum. Brutal, yet gentle. He didn't behave like I expected a cartel member to behave. Sure, he was ruthless, but never with me. I didn't understand. It was almost like he was two people.

"I may not answer, but you can ask."

Well, that didn't sound promising. Still, there were so many things I wanted to know about him.

"What made you join the cartel? I mean, if your brother

is a drug addict, wouldn't that be a reason *not* to become a part of it?"

Tomás was silent for so long, I didn't think he was going to respond. I'd almost given up on getting an answer when he spoke with resignation.

"You don't always have a choice."

His response was cryptic at best. I didn't want to push, but I still wanted to understand.

"Do you ever talk to your brother?"

"Every couple months I visit him, but he asked me to stop coming."

From the way he said the last, I had the impression he didn't mean to say so much.

"Why doesn't he want to see you anymore? I mean, you're his brother."

Tomás' heart beat was strong beneath my hand. I also felt a tension in him. He was uncomfortable with my questions, but I couldn't stop asking them. Even if he didn't answer.

"I blame Preston for her death, and every time I visit, I can never seem to let him forget it. I don't show up with the intention of making him feel guilty, but it always comes out. He makes a snide remark, I make one back, and the next thing you know, we're arguing. My feelings volley between anger and guilt, and I can't stop either one."

I shifted so my chin rested on his chest and looked up at him. "I can understand the anger, but why the guilt?"

Tomás refused to meet my eyes, only stared up at the ceiling. I continued to wait and was soon rewarded for my patience.

He spoke so low I had difficulty hearing him. "Because

I've done the exact things that ruined my brother's life and killed my mother. I'm no better than he is. I'm a fucking hypocrite and the guilt eats away at me."

My heart broke at the desolation in his words. I wanted to assuage his guilt, but there was nothing I could do. Until he let it go, it would continue to fester inside him like a sickness. I could only love him. My breath hitched at the thought. Did I love him? How could I love him already? We barely knew each other. Surely love didn't happen that fast? Especially between two people as different as us.

Instead of platitudes, I tried to show Tomás how wrong he was. I crawled on top of him and kissed him for all he was worth. My fingers threaded through his hair, and I clutched his head tight while I feasted on his mouth. I put every emotion in my kiss, pulling them from the depths of my soul. This unconventional connection between us didn't seem to be dissipating. It burst from me, surrounding us both in its warmth. I didn't want to call it love. I just wanted to savor this feeling of connectedness we had between us, for however long it lasted.

When I'd climbed on top of him, Tomás' hands had auto-matically gripped my waist. As the kiss went on for what seemed like hours, they wandered. Up and down my back until on the trek downward they continued and he grabbed and squeezed my ass, pulling my now soaking wet pussy closer to him. I ached so deep inside, in a place only he could reach. I squealed into his mouth when we rolled and I was suddenly beneath him. He reached out to grasp my hands, interlacing our fingers, before bringing them up to cage my head between our connected limbs. Tomás shifted just slightly, and I spread my legs wider to make room for him. Deepening the kiss, he tilted his head so we fit together like two pieces of a puzzle. His tongue swept through my mouth, and I moaned my pleasure.

Finally, Tomás broke our kiss and stared straight into my eyes, no words spoken between us. With our gazes locked, I felt him shift and reach over to grab one of the condoms I'd set on the nightstand last night. He reached between us to don it and then his cock slid up and down my slit, becoming wet with my juice, until he reached my pussy. He slowly entered me with gentle ease, his eyes never leaving mine. Once he was fully embedded, I wrapped my legs around his waist, and he began to thrust, taking his time, pausing slightly when just the tip was left before pushing back in. With every thrust of his hips I counter thrusted, bringing us as close as two people could get. Every time our pelvises met, the friction increased on my clit.

We continued our dance, until the pressure that had been building exploded and a kaleidoscope of colors burst across my vision. Within seconds, my orgasm rushed over me. On and on tiny tremors continued to pulse until finally my body relaxed.

I unlocked my legs from around Tomás, and he rolled to his back, taking me with him. I cuddled up next to him with my arm across his chest and my head rested on his shoulder. His heartbeat thudded against my hand where it rested on his chest, and I matched my breathing to his. I savored the moment until exhaustion overtook me and I drifted off.

CHAPTER 22

I CALLED Alejandro and let him know I'd be picking him up at nine before heading to the meet. I'd dropped Ines off for her final shift at *SINoritas* before running home to take a quick shower. She'd maintained her cover for a couple more weeks after Ernesto's death to gather more intel on the cartel. When I told her I had to take care of business, she'd become withdrawn. It was a reminder of who I truly was.

I just didn't know if the reminder was for her or me.

Just before nine, I pulled up to Alejandro's condo and honked. When he exited the building, my jaw almost dropped. Gone were the baggy jeans, oversized basketball jersey, and ten pounds of gold around his neck. His hair was styled perfectly, and he was dressed in a tailored designer suit, platinum cuff links, and wing-tipped shoes, like he was about to step foot on a *GQ* magazine photo shoot.

"Nice clothes," I threw out when he'd slid into the passenger's seat.

He shot me a suspicious-looking smile. "Yes, I know."

I glared at him, my instincts warning me something was

about to happen, but for the life of me, I couldn't figure out what it was. My body was buzzing with tension. We passed the rest of the ride in silence. The dislike between Alejandro and I was mutual so we rarely had anything to say to each other, unless it was me lecturing him. When we were almost to our destination, I knew it was time for another lecture.

"Don't forget, follow my lead. Mr. Escobar is a powerful man your uncle is trying to impress. Which means he needs to talk to someone who knows the business like the back of their hand. Not some novice."

"I have a feeling I know more than you think I do."

"Unless some miracle has occurred, then I highly doubt that, Junior."

He sent me a sideways glance and mocking half-smile, but remained silent, before returning his gaze out the passenger window. Finally, we reached the meeting site.

Álvarez owned several abandoned warehouses throughout Chicago. He alternated them, so rarely did we meet at the same place more than once every six to eight months. Less chance of getting caught that way. Several of the warehouses were ones where "interrogations" occurred like with Diego Garcia all those months ago. Others were meeting locales with Miguel's supplier from Mexico.

Raúl Escobar was a member of the Mexican branch of the Juarez Cartel. He was also rumored to be distantly related to Columbian drug lord Pablo Escobar, but I don't know how much truth there was to it. Tonight was meant to be an introductory meeting between Alejandro and Raúl. It was important to Miguel that the relationship between the two begin cultivating now. Trust was the main component of the business agreement between the two leaders. Miguel purchased the drugs and Escobar smuggled them into the country. Once they were delivered, Miguel would then cut it, mixing it with other substances so it was no longer one hundred percent pure. He then sold it for a higher profit margin.

They'd had a profitable working relationship for years, but the Sinaloa cartel, our biggest rival for the drug trade in the States, continued to own more control in the surrounding states. Miguel had been trying for almost a year now to take over the business in those same states, but no matter who he recruited or who he killed, he still hadn't managed to gain the upper hand.

For some reason Miguel thought Alejandro might have better ideas to help further grow the business. Which was why Raúl needed to meet with Alejandro.

The double doors of the warehouse swung open upon our approach. Once I'd pulled all the way in, they closed behind us. I parked the car and both Alejandro and I exited. Next to a black Audi stood Raúl. He, like Miguel, was a quintessential businessman. Unlike Miguel, he didn't take care of himself. He wore an expensive suit with the buttons pulling across the front. A small section of his white half-unbuttoned dress shirt peeked out between the upside down V made by his jacket opening below the last button. Several gold chains lay in a bed of dark, curling chest hair. Which must have been where the hair on his balding head had migrated to. Raúl smiled broadly, and a gold capped front tooth winked at us behind his lips.

"Tomás, how wonderful to see you again," he greeted, arm outstretched for a handshake, the black diamond ring on his finger sparkling in the LED lighting. His jovial attitude always seemed like a conundrum to the vicious cartel leader I knew him to be. I'd once seen him shoot a member of his own organization because Raúl felt he was being disrespected.

"A pleasure as always, Mr. Escobar." I returned his greeting and handshake.

"How many times have I asked you to call me Raúl?"

I merely shrugged. "I've lost count."

He shook his head in a despairing way before changing the topic. "So, how's business?"

"We've tried to gain control of the southeast part of the state, but our competitor has somehow managed to produce a new, more potent product for less. They're turning around and selling it for almost three times what they paid for it. Word on the street is that Emilio Salazar has every intention of bringing his shit into Chicago. Miguel has no intention of letting that happen."

Raúl grunted in disgust. "Salazar has been a thorn in our side for years."

"Has anyone considered snipping the thorn off?"

My head snapped in Alejandro's direction, while Raúl let out a belly laugh.

"Nobody was talking to you, pup."

"No, no, I like how the boy thinks."

"Mr. Esco—Raúl, this is Mr. Álvarez's nephew, Alejandro Ramírez. Miguel has decided it's time for Alejandro to learn how this business is run for when he decides he'd like to retire. There is still a lot he needs to learn. Like when to shut his mouth and listen."

Alejandro stood taller and stepped closer to him. "Oh, I

believe Raúl has seen exactly what it is that I know. *¿No es cierto mi amigo?*

My gaze darted back and forth between the two men. What the hell was going on?

One of Raúl's men stepped up next to him. He turned his head slightly toward him and the man leaned over and whispered in his ear. His body went rigid with tension, and he slowly looked over at me and stared hard. He straightened and threw a look to another one of his men with an almost imperceptible nod. Almost too casually, the man began to move, positioning himself behind me. *What was going on?* I didn't have to wait long to find out. A searing pain shot through my head, and I fell to my knees with a groan.

"The fuck?" God, my head was pounding. I reached up, feeling for blood. Nothing, but I had a huge goose egg. I swallowed back nausea.

I looked up to meet his eyes when he squatted down next to me. My stomach dropped. This was the killer I'd once witnessed.

My cover had been blown.

How'd they find out? Not that it mattered. I was dead either way.

"Héctor just shared with me some extremely disturbing news. He couldn't possibly be correct though, could he?" Raúl's lip curled up in a sneer.

I sat back on my heels, palms on my thighs and tried to remain calm. "Since I have no idea what you're talking about, maybe it would be best if you tell me."

He stood and circled around before standing in front of

me again. Alejandro moved to join him. "What do we have here?"

Raúl unholstered a gun and placed it directly against my forehead. "It would seem our 'friend' here is an undercover D.E.A. agent. Isn't that right?"

I swallowed even as my heart thumped almost out of my chest. He pressed the gun harder which only exacerbated my headache and I couldn't help my groan of pain that escaped. I knew I needed to answer.

"Yes." I confessed, expecting the gun to go off now that my identity was confirmed.

My attention shifted to Alejandro who began laughing hysterically. It took several moments before he brought himself under control. Even Raúl seemed surprised by his reaction. Finally, he cleared his throat. "Oh, this is rich. My uncle has been sharing secrets with the enemy for years and never once suspected."

"How did you find out?"

"Héctor here. It would seem you busted his cousin during a raid several years ago. Héctor was one of the only two who got away. I guess your luck just ran out. Say good-bye, pig."

My eyes closed of their own accord. I didn't want anyone, especially Alejandro, seeing my fear.

"Wait." My eyes popped open at Alejandro's command. "Let's not kill him just yet. I want to be the one to do it. My uncle's time has come."

CHAPTER 23

SQUEALING tires had my body spinning around to find the source. Michele and I were just leaving *SINoritas* after our shift, and under the overhead street lights illuminating the area the familiar black Mercedes with dark-tinted windows came to an abrupt halt. Instinctively, I moved in front of her when Alejandro stepped out from the backseat. Thankfully, there were still a few regulars loitering outside hoping to get one of the girls to go home with him, so, while it may not be large, there was still a crowd. There were also surveillance cameras, which eased my mind only a little.

I hadn't seen him in a few weeks, and he looked different. He wasn't wearing his typical baggy jeans, basketball jersey, and gold chains. And apparently it didn't matter that it was three a.m., he still wore those stupid aviator sunglasses. Instead, he looked like a younger, polished suit-wearing version of his uncle. I didn't know what to make of the change.

"Go back inside and call the police, Michele. Now," I

whispered to her over my shoulder, hoping she heard me over my galloping heartbeat. I had no desire for this girl I'd come to genuinely care about to get hurt.

He strode toward me with a confidence I'd never seen him pull off before. When he finally stood in front of me, he removed his sunglasses and sent me a smile that scared the shit out of me. I'd learned to read his expressions during our time together, and this wasn't one I'd ever seen before.

"Hello, Gabby."

I nodded at his greeting. "Alejandro. What do you want?"

"I wanted to chat with you for a bit." The reptilian smile remained. "Why don't you come with me."

I recognized it wasn't a question. This version of Alejandro made me more nervous than the immature, partying, careless one. That persona was predictable. Manageable. I didn't know who this Alejandro was. I only knew I had no intention of going with him.

"I don't think so. Whatever you have to say to me, you can say right here."

My whole body warned of danger. My heart pounded so loudly I was surprised he couldn't hear it. He looked over my shoulder and my gaze followed his. I breathed a sigh of relief that Michele had apparently listened to me.

Did Alejandro know I was a cop? Was I about to die like my brother? The thought terrified me for so many reasons. My first thought was of my father and brothers.

Then, there was Tomás. I thought of what my death would do to him. Words hadn't been spoken aloud, but no matter how hard I'd fought it, I'd fallen for the man. I wasn't conceited enough to believe he loved me, but there was something there. Every touch. Every kiss. Every breath spoke of greater feelings. We hadn't even scratched the surface of our relationship and now it might be over before it could truly begin.

Well, if my life was about to end, I wasn't going out without a god damn fight. Taking the offensive, since Alejandro seemed to want the silence to draw out until I'd been sufficiently freaked out, I spoke up.

"What did you need to tell me so urgently that you had to drive all the way here in the middle of the night?"

"Brody Thomas." He spat in disgust. "Do you recognize the name?"

"No. Am I supposed to?"

Alejandro studied me intently. Whatever he saw must have satisfied him, because he began to laugh. He laughed until he was almost in tears.

"Oh, Gabby, you really don't know, do you?"

My confusion turned to irritation. "I said I didn't. So, why don't you enlighten me."

He brought himself under control, wiping away a non-existent tear. "For over a month you led me on. Shaking your tits and ass at every opportunity, but then acting like a virgin whenever we were alone together. At first, I thought it was cute how you thought you weren't anything but a whore. In fact, you played the part so well, I almost fell for it."

His jovial attitude melted away until the temperature surrounding me seemed to drop. Alejandro's rage was so ice cold, I actually shivered with it. Where was he going with this? There had to be more to this than a spoiled toddler not getting a piece of ass. Hopefully he'd get to it soon, because this tension in my body was giving me a headache.

Alejandro's gaze became unfocused as though recalling some memory. "I saw you with him. I didn't even know you two knew each other, but when that *cabrón* kissed you, you were practically begging him to fuck you. I knew then that you really were *una puta*. I've been following the two of you for weeks, and you had no idea."

"I don't know who you're talking about."

"Brody Thomas. Or as you know him, Tomás González."

There was only one reason I could think of why someone would be using a pseudonym and working for the cartel.

Alejandro snickered evilly. "Ah-ha. It took you less time to figure it out than I thought it would. You, *mi pequeño coño*, have been fucking an undercover D.E.A. agent."

Holy shit. It all made sense now. I pushed aside the betrayal I felt that Tomás -- Brody -- had hidden his identity from me. He knew I was a police officer. Why hadn't he trusted me enough to tell me? "Does your uncle know?"

He smiled arrogantly, all traces of the Alejandro I thought I knew gone.

"Of course he doesn't. He still thinks Tomás is loyal to him. Remember all those big plans I was telling you about? The time has come. My uncle has become soft. He no longer has what it takes to bring this organization to the top. He's let the Sinaloa Cartel rule for far too long. It's time for a reorganization to happen. That means removing my uncle from his position and any of those who follow him."

There was a hint of evil to his tone. Did he already have

Tomá— Brody held somewhere? Was he being tortured at this exact moment? God, what was I going to do? I was so busy worrying that I didn't see Alejandro move until it was too late. He grabbed me by my hair and yanked me against him. I choked out a gasp. A flash of silver glowed in the street light right before my face ignited like fire. It was overwhelming, and I screamed out in painful agony.

"No one fucks with me. Not some soon-to-be-dead undercover agent and not some useless cunt." He threw me to the ground where I landed on all fours. He spat on me before turning and calmly walking back to the vehicle.

"Gabby!" Michele's yell sounded like it was coming from inside a tunnel. I barely heard her. My entire focus was on the droplets of something dark landing between my hands on the concrete beneath them. Nausea was building, and I swallowed back the vomit. Dimly, I could hear the sound of sirens in the distance and running footsteps getting closer. I pushed upward so I remained on my knees and sat back on my heels.

"Jesus, Gabby." Damon's horrified whisper reached my ears. He hollered in the direction of the club. "Someone get me some clean towels. Now."

My hand reached up toward my face, but he grabbed it, staying my movement. "Don't. Your hands are dirty."

Sobs sounded loudly in my ears and I looked up at Michele who had tears pouring down her cheeks.

Oddly, I now felt numb. "I bet that's gonna leave a mark."

My emotionless comment only made Michele cry harder. I couldn't be sure, but it really felt like the pain was lessening. Or perhaps I was in shock and so high on adrenaline that it only seemed like it. More footsteps sounded and someone handed Damon a pile of towels. More gently than I expected from a man with hands that size, he wiped away the blood still slowly dripping down the side of my face. I hissed when he hit one spot.

"Shit, sorry."

He continued his dabbing and wiping, being extra cautious.

The sirens were now right on top of us and blue lights flashed in the night sky. "Move out of the way, people. Move it."

A flashlight blinded me for a moment before cursing ensued. The patrol officer barked at dispatch through his shoulder comm.

"Miss, can you stand?"

Blindly, I reached out for a hand and was helped to my feet. Thankfully, the shock began to recede and I was coming back to my surroundings. Which also meant my cheek hurt like a mother fucker. I grabbed a clean towel from Damon and placed it against my face. *Fucking Alejandro.* I was going to kill that piece of shit.

"Can you tell us what happened?"

I was saved from responding by the arrival of the ambulance. I knew I was going to have to answer questions, but I'd rather do it later. My identity would be revealed once I got to the hospital, and I needed time to come up with a response that didn't involve bringing Tomás into it. Not until I talked to my family.

Ignoring the cop, I turned to Damon and Michele, who were still waiting on the sidelines.

"Keep her safe."

The command lingered as I let the EMTs load me into the ambulance and we were soon en route to Rush University Medical Center. Knowing I needed a plan, I quickly formulated one, and prayed I stayed alive long enough. I hadn't been able to save my brother, but I'd be damned if I wouldn't save the man I was coming to love.

CHAPTER 24

ONCE I ARRIVED at the hospital, the on-call plastic surgeon had been brought in to stitch my wound. He'd told me I was lucky my assailant hadn't hit any nerves and paralyzed my face. Once he was done, he wrote me a prescription for painkillers while the nurse gave me brief wound care instructions. Then I was free to go. Two uniformed officers greeted me in the waiting room.

"Officer Rodriguez."

So they'd finally discovered my identity.

"Gentlemen." I nodded in greeting.

"We're gonna need your statement."

I let them lead me to their patrol car and transport me to the station. I'd call my *papá* from there. I followed them into an interrogation room and took a seat. Knowing it might be a while before the investigators showed up, I rested my head on my forearms on the table. I was emotionally and physically spent. I must have dozed, because the clearing of a throat woke me. Slightly disoriented, it took me a minute to remember where I was. Until

I spotted the worried face of the man sitting across from me. I started to smile in reassurance, but the ache in my cheek stopped me.

"Hey Pablo."

"Jesus, Ines, what the fuck happened?"

On the ride to the hospital, I'd been glad my brother hadn't been one of the officers who'd shown up. Without a doubt, he would have blown my cover. Unintentional or not.

"Alejandro Ramírez is what happened."

Pablo was the middle child. He was the one who always kept the peace between the five of us. He was level-headed and was slow to anger. So, I was shocked as hell when he picked up the chair and threw it across the room. Papers went flying through the air when he swept them off the table. He raged about how he was going to kill Miguel and Alejandro and no one would ever find their bodies. When there was nothing left to destroy, he stood huffing and puffing in the middle of the room, running his fingers through his hair.

I stood and made my way around the table. I reached up and wrapped my fingers around his forearms, bringing them down to his side. Then I stood on tiptoe and kissed his cheek, whispering in his ear.

"Necesito la ayuda de la familia."

I dropped back down and backed away, taking my former seat. Pablo gave an imperceptible nod. After Pablo took my formal statement about a lover's quarrel, I followed him to his car, and we drove to our father's house in silence. It was after six in the morning, my face was beginning to hurt, and I just wanted to sleep for a few hours.

Pablo parked in the drive and we entered the house together.

"Have the boys meet here at ten. We all need to talk."

I turned and headed to my old room. I didn't even bother undressing before falling on top of the covers. I was asleep before my head even hit the pillow.

Pounding on my door jolted me awake. My whole body ached, but most especially my cheek. Thoughts of last night flashed through my mind. I knew Alejandro would be making his move soon, which meant I needed to act fast. Considering the condition I was in, I knew it was going to be a battle. The pounding started up again.

"I'm coming. Give me a minute."

I rolled out of bed and stumbled to the door. Victor stood on the other side.

"I'm going to fucking kill him."

Twenty-six years later and it was obvious my brothers *still* didn't get me. If anyone was going to kill Alejandro, it was going to be me.

"Is everyone else here?"

"Yes, Manuel just arrived."

"Good," I nodded. "Just give me a few minutes and I'll be out."

He nodded and left me to get ready. I gazed at my reflection in the mirror. Jesus, I looked like shit. My makeup was smeared, my cheek was bruised, crusted with blood, and decorated with blue stitches, and my hair looked like I'd been struck by lightning. I combed it out, brushed my teeth, and tried to wash off as much blood as I could. I was desperate for a shower, but there wasn't time. Slapping on another layer of deodorant, I figured it wasn't going to get any better than this for a little bit.

Alejandro was unpredictable, and I had no idea how much time Brody had left. I only knew I was his only chance at survival. Ever since Alejandro had broken the news to me about Brody, I'd wondered how he'd discovered his identity.

He hadn't figured out who I was.

To him, I was some *puta* who didn't have a brain in her head. I was arm candy. Someone he could show off to his friends. I didn't cause problems. I was an ornament. There was no way I was any type of threat. You didn't just grow up thinking less of women, that shit was taught, and considering he was raised by his uncle, I knew Miguel held the same view of women. That particular viewpoint had given me a distinct advantage. One I fully planned on continuing to use.

I had no idea where Alejandro might be keeping Brody, but I needed to figure it out fast. Which meant I needed to play the same role I'd been playing. Only better. I headed to the kitchen where my father and brothers gathered and paced. They all had that pissed off look, especially when they saw my face. I withdrew a bottle of acetaminophen from the cabinet and downed several pills with a glass of water. Then, I took my regular seat at the table. The boys all followed suit.

"Pablo says you need our help." My father broke the silence.

"*Sí, papá.* You're not going to like it, but you have to trust me."

"Tell us what's going on, *conejito.*"

"Alejandro Ramírez is planning a coup."

Other than shocked looks, they remained silent. Now, came the hard part of my confession.

"For the last few weeks, I've been involved in an affair with Tomás González, a man who works for Miguel Álvarez."

With that pronouncement, they all started talking at once. Various choruses of "what the fuck were you thinking?" My father slammed his fist on the table.

"*Silencio.*"

They quieted down, with a few grumbles remaining. My father nodded at me to continue. I swallowed hard before beginning.

"Last night, this morning, whenever, Alejandro confronted me about the affair. I believe he gave me this—" I gestured to the cut he'd made, "—as punishment for being with Tomás. He didn't take too kindly to the perceived betrayal. I never slept with Alejandro and he took this as a personal affront. To him, I'm a worthless whore. Tomás, on the other hand, is a key player in his takeover. Alejandro has taken him prisoner and plans on using him to taunt his uncle. To lord over Miguel that he knew Tomás' secret from the beginning."

I stared at the table, rubbing my fingers in my lap, sick over what Alejandro was doing to Tomás. No, to Brody.

"What is Tomás' secret, Ines?" This came from Manuel.

I looked up at four pairs of eyes so similar to mine. My heart ached for the missing pair. I plunged forward.

"The man Miguel calls Tomás González doesn't exist. His real name is Brody Thomas, and he's an undercover D.E.A. agent."

"Holy shit, they'll kill him."

I flinched. My father caught my eye, and he must have seen something there.

"You didn't know about this until Alejandro crowed over his knowledge, did you?"

I shook my head. "He never told me, even after he found out I was a cop."

Pablo's brow creased in confusion. "You're saying this Tomás, or Brody person knew you were with the police. How did he find out?"

I took a slow, deep breath in before answering. "He was there when Ernesto was killed. I believe Ernesto told him."

This set my brothers off again. While they raged, I rose from my seat and moved toward my father. I lowered myself to my knees, and grasping his hand in mine, I brought it up to my lips. I kissed it before laying it against my unmarked cheek. I stared up at him, beseechingly.

"*Lo amo, papá.*" *I love him,* I confessed. "We're his only hope. *Por favor.*"

CHAPTER 25

It had taken an hour to convince my family to move forward with my plan. Now, I just prayed it worked. I quickly took a shower while everyone else gathered all the ammunition and firepower they could get their hands on. We all knew our destination, but we each took a different route to get there. Then, they all waited while I set everything in motion. I pulled into the drive, stopping when I reached the iron gate and gate house. It was my first time visiting this house by myself. I'd always accompanied Alejandro, but since we hadn't been together for weeks, I had no idea how I'd be received.

I had a feeling neither the Alejandro I met last night nor the one I thought I knew would want it to become common knowledge that he couldn't even keep a stripper as a girlfriend so the chances that I was banned from the property were pretty close to nil. I was about to find out.

The security guard stepped out of the gate house and bent down to speak through my open window. "Miss Lòpez, I'm sorry, but Alejandro isn't here."

I couldn't see his eyes behind the sunglasses, but I could feel him staring at the stitches on the side of my face.

"I'm actually here to speak with Mr. Álvarez. It's extremely important."

He stepped away and back into the gate house. I could see him speaking to someone through a walkie talkie. My grip tightened on the steering wheel and I tried to control my breathing. I let out a small whimper of relief when the large gate creaked and moaned and slowly began to open. I gave the guard a small wave before entering the devil's lair. I parked my car and strode up the steps, the front door swinging open before my foot hit the top one.

Miguel's housekeeper, Maria Consuela, greeted me. She frowned when she saw me, but otherwise didn't react.

"Señor Álvarez está afuera."

I nodded my thanks and headed out to the courtyard where I'd already discovered Miguel spent most of his time. It was the first visit where I wasn't able to appreciate the beauty of the home Miguel had built. Exposed wood, arches entryways, earthy colors with differing shades of red, orange, and yellow, with the occasional pop of blue were seen throughout the house. I'd never pictured him as being particularly religious, but several paintings of the Virgin Mary were located throughout the house, as well as few crosses and rosaries. The floor was a reddish-orange terra cotta and there were several bright scatter rugs in different rooms. It bespoke of his strong familial ties to his Mexican heritage.

I exited the French doors and the almost tropical air beneath the trees was warming. I wove through the courtyard and when it opened up to the pool area, I spotted

Miguel seated under an umbrella at a table near the pool, dressed in a dark, pinstriped designer suit like always. The days were beginning to get hotter, and I had no idea how he could stand wearing nothing else. He never appeared to sweat or look like he was ever in discomfort. Every strand of dark hair was swept back off his forehead and his suits were always perfectly pressed. It was like nothing could touch him. He was speaking to someone on the phone, but he smiled and waved me over. Confidently, with my head high and shoulders back, I made my way over to him. His smile faded, the closer I got.

"*Te llamaré mas tarde.*" He hung up the phone after his promise to call the person back later. He set the phone on the table and stood. He moved around the side of the table, his arms out in front of him. I let him grasp my hands in his.

"*Dios mio*, child, who did this to you? Does this have anything to do with the urgent need to see me?"

Let the charade begin.

"Alejandro is planning on killing you and taking over your organization."

He dropped my hands like they'd burned him, and his face froze like granite. Rage brewed in his eyes.

"Tell me how you know this."

"Over the last few months, he has been hinting to me that he had big plans. We'd go to the club a lot and he would disappear with several of his friends. I don't know what they talked about. I only know he was different when he returned. I couldn't have been the only one who noticed it."

I paused for a moment to let him ponder my words. Make him question Alejandro's behavior over the last few months. Of course, everything I was spewing was bullshit, but it was enough to get Miguel thinking. Growing up with four brothers, I learned that if you wanted them to do something, you needed to play it well enough that they thought it was their idea to begin with.

"Last night I was leaving *SINoritas* when Alejandro approached me. He started bragging about knowing a secret. About how stupid you were to have not figured it out. How you were obviously not fit to run the family business if you let a traitor in your most intimate circle and didn't even realize it. How you've let the Sinaloa Cartel rule for too long."

Miguel grabbed my arm and squeezed so hard I knew he'd leave finger shaped bruises on my skin. I flinched and tried to pull out of his grip, but he was too strong.

"What traitor?"

Through clenched teeth, I choked out, "I don't know. I assumed he was talking about himself."

He shook me like a rag doll, I swear my brain rattled in my head. "You lie!"

"No, I swear. Please! You're hurting me."

He released me and began to pace. I clutched my arm, trying to ease the pain.

"When I told him he was too weak to overthrow you, he gave me this." I flashed him the left side of my face. "I think he would have done more if someone hadn't called the police. But before he left, he told me your time was coming."

He remained silent while he continued to pace. My whole body was tense, my fingers ached from clenching them into a fist, and I could feel beads of sweat running down my back.

"Where is *mi sobrino* now?"

"I don't know. I haven't seen him since he left the club last night. He didn't think I'd have the nerve to come to you. But, after doing this to me, he deserves whatever's coming to him."

Miguel's smile was so sinister, the hairs on the back of my neck stood on end and gooseflesh pebbled on my arms. This was the face behind one of the most powerful cartels in the world. A man who wouldn't hesitate to kill a man who wronged him. I *almost* felt sorry for Alejandro. Because nephew or not, Alejandro didn't have much time left on this earth. No one fucked with Miguel Álvarez.

"Oh, Alejandro is going to get exactly what's coming to him."

He pulled out his phone, and leaving me standing there, he headed toward the house. I knew I'd been dismissed. Shortly after Miguel entered the house, I followed. I retraced my path through the house, a raised voice coming from behind a closed door, and let myself out. I got into my car and headed out to the main road to wait. I quickly called my father.

"Everything went according to plan as far as I can tell. Miguel was on the phone when I left. Now, we wait. See where he goes."

"Are you all right, *conejito*?" I heard the worry in his tone.

"I'm fine, *papá*. He didn't hurt me. I'm just worried about Brody. I keep imagining every worst case scenario." I bit back tears. They wouldn't do Brody or me any good.

"We'll find him Ines. I promise."

My father's words had me feeling marginally better. He'd never made me a promise he hadn't kept. He wasn't going to start now. In the background, I heard the click and static sound of a comm unit. Then, Victor's voice.

"Miguel's on the move."

Each of my brothers had stationed themselves on various streets surrounding Miguel's home. That way we knew which way he went. Each car would randomly take over following him until he reached his destination. We only hoped it was where Alejandro and Brody were located.

CHAPTER 26

I SPIT out blood after the next strike to my face. One of my eyes was swollen shut, I'd felt a couple ribs crack, and my tongue wiggled several loose teeth. Javier had a fucking mean left hook. I'd been truly shocked when I discovered that he'd turned against Miguel and joined forces with Alejandro. "A new generation to bring about change," he'd said. I don't know what kind of fucking change he thought Alejandro planned on bringing, but Javier clearly thought whatever it was, was worth it.

I was in some cabin, strung up by my hands to a chain hanging from the ceiling, my shoulders and arms completely numb at this point. I was pretty sure there was also some nerve damage. If Alejandro was going to kill me, I wished he'd hurry up and get it over with.

"How are you feeling Brody?"

I glared at him out of my good eye. "Never better."

He laughed like I'd said something hilarious. "Yes, I can see that. Although, you do appear to be in a slight predicament. Whatever will you do?"

I returned his smile with one of my own, bloodied as it was. "I'm sure I'll figure something out."

He huffed out another laugh. "You always have thought you were smarter than me. But, I guess you were wrong. Just look at you. Strung up like a puppet. And I'm your puppeteer. I bet you never saw this day coming. I mean, all this time and none of you ever guessed what I'd been planning. Not you and certainly not my pathetic uncle. You only ever saw what I wanted you to see."

Alejandro pulled a chair over, swung it around and straddled it, resting his forearms across the back. He then laid his chin on his arms and half-smiled. I kept quiet, letting him run off at the mouth.

"You never even realized I was leading you to all those drugs busts you were making behind my uncle's back. All those "tips" you passed off to your superiors? They all came from me. Because for every measly bust you made, I was pulling off bigger deals while you were otherwise occupied. I was building my empire. All the dealers my uncle refused to supply, I helped. They're all now loyal to me. That's what happens when you underestimate someone. I guess you're not some badass super-agent now are you?"

Alejandro had returned early this morning telling me that something big was about to go down, but wouldn't elaborate. His phone had been ringing non-stop for the last hour, but after glancing at the caller ID, he'd ignored almost all of them. He looked entirely too self-satisfied. Periodically, he'd given orders for Javier to deal out some more punishment. He obviously didn't have the balls to throw any punches himself.

"I'm still less of a pussy than you."

That got a chuckle out of Javier. Practically foaming at the mouth, Alejandro jumped up from his seated position, simultaneously tossing the chair out of his way, and took two steps toward me, sucker punching me right in the gut. I groaned and coughed up more blood, almost puking in the process. Served my dumb ass right for taunting the little shit. Still worth it though. Pissed off people made mistakes. I needed him to come a little closer. I was ready to wrap my legs around his neck and choke the asshole to death.

"Fuck you, Brody. Oh, that's right, the *pequeño coño* already did that. Did I tell you I paid her a little visit last night?"

"You better not have touched her, motherfucker." I coughed out, spitting up more blood.

Heedless of the agony in my arms, I jerked and yanked at the bindings holding me, my body thrashing as I tried to work them loose. Alejandro's sinister laugh mocked my efforts. He pulled a knife out from behind his back and turned it blade up, blade down, the overhead lights reflecting off the silver while his eyes followed its movement.

"She got a small taste of this. You should have seen her bleed." He continued as though I hadn't even spoken. "She's not so pretty anymore. When I'm king, I plan on paying her another visit. I bet she has the sweetest pussy. First, I'm going to fuck it raw and then I'm going to slit her throat. Or maybe I'll slit her throat and then fuck her. I haven't decided yet. Tell me, Brody. How does that pussy taste?"

Despite his words, or maybe because of them, a calmness entered me. It was intense and overwhelming. I stopped struggling, all pain forgotten, as a hatred so pure entered me. I looked right at Alejandro and spoke with deadly intent. "I'm going to kill you. It may not be today, or even tomorrow. But I promise, I *am* going to kill you."

The temperature in the room dropped at the iciness coming from me. I hadn't lied to him. The reckoning was coming, and Alejandro was going to pay for whatever he'd done to Ines. My gaze never left his, and he must have read the truth in them, because he shifted nervously, no longer the cocky piece of shit he was moments ago.

"Good—" his voice cracked on the word. He cleared his throat and began again. "—good luck with that."

I merely continued to stare, not blinking. He quickly looked away and took a step back. The sound of a car on gravel broke the tension. Alejandro darted a glance at Javier.

"Are you expecting someone?"

Javier shook his head. "Just you."

Alejandro moved to the window and moved the curtain aside to peek outside. "Well, well, well, it looks like my uncle has decided to pay us a visit. I wonder what he could want?"

I started laughing despite the pain. "Looks like maybe *you're* not as smart as you thought you were."

He took five long strides toward me and backhanded me across the face. "Shut your mouth."

His strike loosened a tooth, and I spit out more blood. Against the pain, I gave a smile. "You hit like a little bitch."

Before he could hit me again a knock sounded on the door. Without waiting for a response, it swung open, and in stepped Miguel, dressed to the nines in his pinstriped designer suit and wing tip shoes. Right on his heels was José Perez, Miguel's second-in-command.

"*Hola, mi sobrino.*" Miguel greeted a little too nonchalantly.

"*Tio*. What brings you here?"

Miguel began to move, circling the room with slow, confident strides, his hands clasped behind his back. I saw the tension in the lines of his arms and knew his relaxed pose was a façade. No matter how cunning Alejandro thought he was, *this* was a man who was meant to be in charge.

He stopped near me, and my breathing slowed while I waited to see what he would do. When he merely moved away and began another trek around the room, I started breathing normally again. I still remained wary and alert, my attention bouncing between Miguel and José, who'd remained by the door, arms crossed over his chest.

"I heard some disturbing news today, and I came to find out whether it was true or not. I didn't realize you owned this cabin. You've never invited me here before. I wonder why that is?"

"It was a recent purchase," Alejandro responded calmly.

Miguel made a non-committal noise. "I see. And why is it you haven't answered your phone? I've been trying to reach you for well over an hour now."

His question was deceptively innocent. Apparently, Alejandro wasn't ready to reveal himself yet, because he adopted his former persona, attempting to look appropriately chastised. "Sorry, *tio*. I must have forgot to turn it off vibrate. I was actually about to call you. But, if you're here, I wonder if you heard the same disturbing news I have."

"And what is that?"

He gestured in my direction. "There's a traitor in your midst."

Miguel steepled his fingers and tapped them against his lips. "Ah, yes, a traitor. I may have heard something about that. It makes me wonder why Tomás is here, especially in his current condition."

I watched the interplay between the two, trying to puzzle out how Miguel discovered Alejandro's betrayal. Was Ines involved somehow? Is that why she'd been harmed? Had she found out the truth and approached Miguel? Discreetly as possible even though every move was pure agony, and still knowing it was useless, I attempted to free myself.

Alejandro sent a look of mock surprise. "Why, he's your traitor. Dearest *tio*, may I present D.E.A. agent Brody Thomas."

CHAPTER 27

WE'D FOLLOWED Miguel through Chicago and onto the highway. I had no idea where we were going. For over an hour, we drove further and further away from the city, until finally his vehicle took an exit, and I realized he was heading toward Fox Lake. I was the last car and far enough behind that I could take the same exit and not seem suspicious. In the meantime, my father and brothers continued straight ahead and planned on backtracking. I stayed a fair distance back until I saw the Mercedes turn down a road. I kept going and radioed Pablo.

"He just turned right onto Wilson Road. Not sure where he's headed though."

"I'm coming up on it, now. I also have the area pulled up on satellite. The road dead ends right at the lakeshore. It looks like there's several old cabins there. Running some data now. I don't know if they're inhabited or not."

Well, at least now we knew the general vicinity.

Pablo's staticky voice came across the bandwidth. "The road dead ends so they're not going anywhere. There's a copse of forest surrounding the cabins. There's a service road about a mile from the house that runs into the trees. I say we park there and hoof it."

"Roger that."

Within ten minutes, we were all parked at the dead end of the road. Victor opened the trunk of his car and started pulling out Kevlar vests. Once we were covered, we gathered all our firearms, strapping holsters on belts, packing pockets with ammunition, and started our hike. Manuel, who was a member of S.W.A.T. and had brought A/V equipment, halted us about ten minutes later. Quietly, and working in unison, we began circling the house, looking for evidence of what was going on inside and a safe entry point. Victor and I positioned ourselves, guns drawn, at the back door on the south side, my father on the west side at a bedroom window, Pablo on the north side at the front entrance, and Manual on the east side at the kitchen window. To our knowledge, the only people inside were Alejandro, Brody, and Miguel, but we needed to be sure before storming in. I couldn't take the chance that there were some extra guests and risk Brody's life.

Static sounded in my earpiece and then Manuel's voice came over the line.

"I've got a visual through the kitchen window. Five males present. Ramírez and an unknown male on south side of living room. Álvarez and Perez on north side of room. Victim in middle of room hanging by arms from ceiling. Conscious but injured."

I ignored Manuel calling Brody a victim, and instead focused on the fact that there were two extra people in there. What I didn't know was if mystery man number four was on Miguel's or Alejandro's side. However, based on positioning, I'd guess he was with the latter.

"No weapons in sight at the moment."

It didn't matter that we couldn't see them. I knew for a fact that José would be armed, and I could only assume, based on prior visual confirmation, that Alejandro had a gun as well.

"Can you get sound in there? We need to know what's being said."

"Roger that. Give me a few minutes."

I waited tensely while my brother worked on getting us ears in the house. I had to trust that he could work his magic and get us more intel. The fact that Brody was alive was the most important thing. Static and crackling voices burst through my ear. It took a few moments before finally, the static settled and the voices became clear. Immediately, I recognized Miguel's baritone.

"There were rumblings that I was making a mistake by bringing you in, but I ignored them because we are *la familia*. Your mother was my sister. I promised her I would raise you like my own and *this is how you repay me*? By attempting to take me out? By destroying everything I've worked so hard to build?"

The calm tone behind Miguel's words didn't fool me. I wondered if Alejandro heard the strength behind them? Miguel was no one's fool. Nephew or not, Miguel would never forgive this betrayal. I craned my neck to listen more closely when Alejandro spoke.

"I'm not destroying anything. I'm making the Juarez cartel more powerful. Something you've failed to do. Instead, you've let the Sinoala cartel run us out of our own territories. You've become so weak that you didn't even know you had this traitor in your midst. *I* was the one who discovered his betrayal. *I* was the one who captured him. You have become complacent, and it's time a new regime took over."

I could imagine the scene. Alejandro in his condescension and cockiness. Miguel, however, had been part of this business for longer than Alejandro had been alive. He'd never seen the inside of a prison, because he was fucking smart.

More static crackled in my ear and then Manuel's voice boomed out loud and clear. "Ramírez pulled a gun on Álvarez."

My stomach dropped. "Damn it. I'm going in."

A chorus of warnings echoed in my ear, but I disregarded them all.

Before Victor could stop me, I kicked in the back door, trusting my brothers to have my back. I heard my brother curse behind me.

Gun drawn, I stormed into the living room. "Freeze. Chicago P.D.. Drop your weapons and put your hands where I can see them."

All four men jerked in my direction, hands reaching for their guns. I swept my arm back and forth between all of them in warning.

"I wouldn't do that if I were you."

My eyes briefly darted to where Brody hung, but I quickly moved my gaze back to Alejandro, still holding his gun, even if he'd lowered it slightly. I felt Victor move in behind me at the same time the front door burst open and my father and two other brothers raced in with guns drawn.

His eyes dragged up and down my body, and that smarmy, shit-eating grin I hated so much appeared on his face.

"Well, well, well. Isn't this a surprise? It looks like you're not just some worthless *puta* after all."

I answered with my own condescending grin. "I guess not. Just think, after all this time, you never figured out that I was an undercover cop. Who looks like a dumbass now?"

Alejandro's cocky grin disappeared and rage crossed his face, his arm moving slightly then stopping like he was itching to shoot me. Like a chameleon, his expression instantly changed again. Back to arrogant. He glanced over at Brody and with an evil twist to his lips, practically snarled.

"Poor, poor Brody. I wonder if he knows you're just my sloppy seconds. That I know exactly what a sweet little pussy you have. How tight it is. How you screamed out my name when I fucked you from behind. You rode my cock like the whore you are."

I blinked. Then I belly laughed until I was almost in tears.

"Oh, you stupid, stupid boy. Do you really think Brody is going to believe you? Not one time have you and I ever fucked. And if you're thinking that first night we met at the club, when I spent the night, you're wrong. I drugged your sorry ass and you passed out within five minutes. You've *never* had this 'sweet, little pussy' you worthless piece of shit."

CHAPTER 28

WHEN INES CAME CRASHING through the back door, I couldn't believe it. Especially when four men followed her in. I drank in the sight of her. Holy shit, she was badass. She looked entirely in her element with her black leathers, Kevlar vest, and 9 mm Glock pulled. She charged in here like she owned the fucking place. Regardless, I was terrified she was going to get hurt. All because of me. When she turned, I saw the stitches down the side of her face. Hatred burned through me like wildfire. I could almost feel it sizzling inside my veins like that first shot of heroin. Alejandro was going to fucking pay. I needed to bide my time. I also wanted her to know I was okay, but the less distraction I offered, the better off she'd be, so I remained still, no matter the agony in my arms and loathing in my soul.

A slow, dramatic clapping had me jerking my head to the left. Miguel, whose presence I couldn't believe I'd almost forgotten, gave one final clap before clasping his hands together against his stomach.

"*¡Bravo mi sobrino!* You've somehow managed to get two undercover cops under one roof. I didn't think it was possible for someone to be a complete and utter fuck up, but this, right here?" Miguel shook his head mockingly. "This is why *I* am the leader of this organization and you're only playing at it. *You* led them all here with your ignorance. *You* will be the one that goes to prison for his *incompetencia. Eres un imbécil. Estupido.* You want to be powerful? You think you can run this organization, and yet you can't even do a single thing right."

Throughout his speech, I wanted to warn Ines, but all eyes were on Miguel. None of them, including Alejandro, noticed what was happening. But I did. I knew exactly what Miguel was doing, and that was pushing all of Alejandro's buttons. Pushing him past control. I'd been working, in some capacity, for Miguel for five years. I knew him. I'd studied him. Right now, he was forcing a fatal reaction, and based on Alejandro's beet-red face, flared nostrils, and heavy breathing, it was working.

"A fuck up? I was the one who cultivated relationships you couldn't begin to. I was making deal after deal, while you sat back and let Emilio Salazar make you a laughing-stock. You haven't even realized the number of your employees who are actually working—" Alejandro pounded his own chest with his fist, "—for me."

Miguel snorted in disdain. "Making deals? Is that what you think you were doing? Child's play. Because for every employee you think has turned their loyalties to you, there are two more who think you are nothing but a worthless *pendejo. No eres nadie.* You are *nothing.*"

I saw the change in Alejandro. The final button had been

pushed. The shift in his eyes and the muscle twitch. I guessed his intention, and at the same time Alejandro raised his gun and aimed it at Miguel, I roared out a warning. "Don't shoot!"

It was too late. Gunfire rang out, and I waited for any number of bullets to strike me. Multiple rounds were fired. I flinched at the sound, knowing at least one of them was meant for me. When the last echo faded, I took stock of my body. No new aches or pains seemed to appear when I moved. The silence was thick and deadly.

I searched out Ines and found her standing near the same spot she'd previously occupied, her gun aimed at someone on the floor. I didn't see any blood on her, but it was hard to tell with the black leather she wore. She didn't seem to be in any pain. I took another look around and saw three bodies on the ground. Wait, where was Miguel? My eyes darted around the room, but still nothing.

"Is everyone okay? Talk to me you guys." I identified the source of the shaky question. It belonged to the man I immediately identified as Ines' father. Dark brown hair with flecks of gray and her chocolate eyes, only his were feverish and over-bright as they darted hastily around the room, checking on the safety of all his children.

"I'm hit, but it's just a flesh wound." He rushed over to the injured man, immediately checking on the wound.

"These two are dead." A brother confirmed.

Ines stepped toward the final body. Alejandro's. His gun lay next to him and she kicked it away. Staying alert, she nudged him with her foot. He groaned in response. The amount of blood pooling beneath his body indicated how seriously he was injured. She squatted and rolled him over.

His breathing sounded wet, and blood spilled from his mouth.

One of her brothers ran over and ripped open his shirt. Blood was everywhere. He applied pressure while another brother called out, "Paramedics are on their way."

Alejandro's eyes fluttered open.

"*Tio?*" He spat out blood with his question. His eyes slowly closed again and with one final raspy exhalation, he was gone.

Eyes scanned the room and Ines' father raced outside. I shifted, intense pain shot up my arms, and I choked out a distressed sound.

"Brody!" Ines screamed just as she raced over to me, patting me down, causing a small moan, no matter how gentle her hands were. "Were you hit? Talk to me, please."

"I'm okay."

She shouted over her shoulder. "Victor, help me get him down."

"Where's Miguel?" I needed to know. Had he escaped during the melee? If so, how?

"I don't know. All of my attention was on Alejandro."

Just then, her brother, Victor, slid to a stop in front of us and began sawing away at my bindings. I screamed in agony when the rope was severed and my arms fell, one out of the socket, causing me to stumble. Ines caught me and helped me stay on my feet. The pain was so great, I wretched and vomited up nothing but bile. I swayed and almost passed out, but I gritted my teeth and willed the darkness away by sheer force.

"Here, sit down." This came from Victor as he and Ines helped me over to the couch. I collapsed against the sofa, still seeing spots. I steadied my breathing and they blessedly began to disappear. My entire body ached, and I was exhausted. Seeing that shit was being handled, I couldn't help but lay my head back and just close my eyes. Bloodflow was returning to my hands and they burned with pins and needles and eight of my ten fingers were numb. But I was alive.

"Drink this." I peered out of my good eye to see Ines's brother with a glass of water. I never even heard him move away, I was that out of it. I nodded my thanks. I struggled to hold onto the cup, but clumsily managed to bring it to my mouth without spilling it down the front of me. I hadn't realized how thirsty I was until the wetness hit my throat. I swallowed the liquid so fast, I almost choked on it.

"Slowly. Take your time."

Once the glass was empty, he took it out of my hand. Then I looked over at Ines. Tears streaked down her face and she was biting her lower lip like she was holding back from a major meltdown. I hated seeing her so defeated. We survived. Against the pain, I reached out and cupped her jaw, rubbing my thumb alongside the cut on her cheek, but not touching it.

"I'm so sorry Ines. I never meant for you to be hurt." My throat was raw.

She covered my hand with hers, and leaned into my touch, but she only continued to cry.

"The Mercedes is gone." Ines' father had returned. "How the fuck did we lose him?"

The brother who'd tried to help Alejandro responded. "When that first gunshot rang out, it was chaos from there. I was trying not to get shot, and protect you guys at the same time. Fucker must have slipped out then."

"Son of a bitch."

The faint sound of sirens floated through the house. Suddenly, a buzzing filled my ears and black spots danced in front of me. My body felt heavy and lethargic. I recognized the signs of adrenaline crash and knew it was about ready to be lights out for me.

"I don't feel so great." My mouth didn't seem to be working right, and my words sounds garbled like they were coming from a tunnel.

"Brody!" Ines screamed at the same time I could feel myself begin to sway. I tried to shake away the cobwebs, but they were winning. I needed to tell her something before everything went dark. Shit, what was it? Oh, yeah.

"Love…" My voice faded and the blackness took over.

CHAPTER 29

I SPENT two nights in the hospital with a dislocated shoulder and some minor nerve damage resulting in numbness and tingling down my arm and fingers, probably for the rest of my life, according to the doctors. They were actually surprised it wasn't worse. I'd also suffered a bruised spleen, dehydration, and I had several loosened teeth that the dentist wasn't sure wouldn't need pulled eventually. All things considering, I didn't think I was too bad off.

Ines' brother Victor stopped by a few times to visit me. We'd talked some and learned we had a few things in common like our love of baseball, including the Colorado Rockies. He was someone I could call a friend eventually. We'd also tiptoed around certain topics. Like why Ines hadn't come to see me. It wasn't because she didn't care.

She needed time to process everything, and no matter how hard it was on me, I needed to respect that. I'm sure it was equally hard, if not more so, on her. She'd been taken completely unaware by my identity, and I knew she was coming to grips with it, and the knowledge that because of who I was, Alejandro had scarred her for life. I only prayed she understood why I kept it from her.

I also made my official statement to the police. With all the evidence I'd been collecting while undercover, I had compiled enough to almost destroy the entire organization. I gave them supplier names, including Raúl Escobar's, all the information regarding warehouses owned by Miguel, businesses used as a front for money laundering, which club's back rooms were used to house Miguel's drug labs. They raided all of them, made hundreds of arrests, and shut down every single business. It would take years for Miguel to rebuild.

I'd arrived home about an hour ago, and my arm was fucking killing me regardless of the sling I wore. The last dose of pain meds had been six hours ago. I'd just reached for the bottle when a knock sounded at my door. My stomach tightened, then dropped when I saw who stood on the other side. When I opened it, I tried not to let my disappointment show when a tall, leggy blonde walked in and not the caramel-haired beauty I'd hoped it was. I had a feeling I knew why she was here.

Landon strolled past me and headed straight to my kitchen. She huffed in disgust at finding the fridge empty. What did she expect? I hadn't lived here full-time in years, and I'd barely wiped my feet on the welcome mat before she'd come barging in. She closed the fridge door and headed to the couch where she flopped down, making herself comfortable, arm splayed across the back of it.

"Word on the street is Álvarez headed back to Mexico. I assume he's licking his wounds. For now anyway. Jesus, Brody. What the hell happened in there?"

I sighed. "I'd taken Alejandro to a deal with Escobar. An introductory meeting if you will. Shit went south when one of Raúl's men recognized me from a drug bust years ago. Suddenly it was lights out, and the next thing I know, I'm waking up to getting my ass handed to me by one of Miguel's, well, I guess Alejandro's, men."

When I'd first gone undercover, I'd been paired up with some dickweed handler who'd rubbed me the wrong way. There wasn't anything specific that made me not trust him, but this was my life. I wasn't comfortable with him, so I called my superiors. It had taken some major cajoling, but they finally reassigned someone else to me. That someone was Ms. Landon Roberts. A rookie. She'd only been with the organization for a year, but she'd graduated at the top of her training class at Quantico. Immediately, I knew she was going places. She wasn't a ballbuster, but she evoked confidence and class. We'd been together ever since. I trusted her implicitly.

"What a fucking nightmare. So, your cover was blown. How does Officer Rodriguez factor in to the showdown at the cabin? Aside from the obvious fact you're fucking her."

She held up her hand when I growled. "Don't be so touchy. You know what I mean."

When I settled, I let her in on everything that had gone down since the last time we'd made contact. I rubbed my free hand down my pants, gearing myself up for possible life in prison. I had to come clean though. No matter how ugly it was.

"After Ramírez confronted Ines, he taunted her with the knowledge he held me captive. He also left her with a life-long memento of my betrayal. She, in turn, went to Álvarez, and told him of Ramírez's plan to take him out and gain control of the cartel. She and her brothers followed Álvarez to the destination where I was being held. He confronted his nephew about the allegations and an argument ensued. Álvarez baited Ramírez enough that he attempted to gun down his uncle. Ines and her brothers entered the house, and multiple shots were fired which led to the death of José Perez, Javier Oca, and Alejandro Ramírez. Miguel Álvarez escaped, as you already know."

Landon sighed in frustration and her head dropped back while she stared at the ceiling for a moment before returning her gaze to me. "I got your letter of resignation. What's that all about, Brody?"

This was the hardest part. I took a deep breath for courage. "I can't go back to the organization. Not after everything I've seen and done. Plus, I don't belong there anymore. It no longer feels right."

She laid her hands in her lap and looked at me in understanding. "Brody, you were undercover. No one can fault you for doing things that weren't quite above board in order to maintain your cover. It's all part of the job. It's often unavoidable, and for the most part, we look the other way when it happens."

Finally, I took a seat in the opposing chair, my good elbow resting on my knee. "I killed someone."

Her response was to blink. And blink again. Her expression turned to understanding. "Diego Garcia. That was your in all those months ago. I assumed—"

"Paulo Hernandez."

With those two words, she inhaled a gasp and stopped

talking. Stopped moving. In fact, I felt like the whole world stopped. Slowly, her eyes widened with realization.

"Oh fuck. Brody." Her words were a whisper. Then, silence. We sat there, neither of us speaking for a few minutes. Finally, Landon cleared her throat.

"Tell me what happened."

"He was the one who murdered Ines' brother."

The whole story poured out of me. She listened intently, never once interrupting. After I finished, I sat back in my chair, exhausted, and waited for judgment.

"Who else knows?" Her voice came out soft.

"Ines. And now you." I was so weary.

"No one else can ever know, Brody. Not now. Not ever."

Wait, what?

"Landon, you understand that your silence makes you complicit to murder?"

"My father suffered from mental illness. For as long as I could remember."

I sat there a minute, confused, wondering what that had to do with anything. "Land—"

She interrupted me. "He would fall into the deepest depression, and nothing I did could shake him from his despair. It would last anywhere from a few days to a few weeks. His melancholy was tangible, Brody. I'd walk into the house after coming home from school, and I could literally *feel it* in the air. It was overpowering, smothering. It tore our family apart."

She paused, inhaling deeply, her eyes focused on the past. I remained silent, waiting to discover where this was going.

"About a year after my parents divorced, I went to spend

a week with my dad that summer. I'd just turned thirteen. The second day I was there, he sent me down the block to the convenient store for some candy. When I got home and stepped into the house, I knew something was wrong. I started up the stairs, my feet growing heavier with each step I took. I moved down the hall to my father's room, where the door was cracked open."

Her voice broke, but she cleared her throat and continued a story I wasn't sure I wanted to hear.

"I saw the blood first. My father's body second. The gun in his hand last. At first glance, I thought he was dead. His face was half blown off. But then he said my name. I mean, I think it was my name. To this day, I still can't be sure, the word was so garbled. I dropped to my knees next to him. Slowly, like it pained him greatly, he reached for my hand. He then placed it on top of his other hand, the one that still held the gun. There was so much sadness in his eyes. So much suffering. Behind all that though, was a small measure of peace fighting its way to the forefront. I couldn't ignore it. Didn't want to ignore it. He tried to raise our connected hands and the gun, but was too weak. So, I helped him. Together our arms moved and with a final I love you, my finger squeezed the trigger."

My mouth tasted like sawdust while Landon swiped at her eyes. They were puffy and bloodshot when she finally turned to look at me. I had no words. Silently, while I continued to sit there in shock, she rose from the sofa and headed to the door. She opened it and then turned slightly toward me, looking over her shoulder.

"To an outsider, what each of us has done is an unpardonable sin. But there are times when you do unpardonable things out of love. Whether it's right or wrong isn't for anyone but a greater power to judge. I'll let the Deputy Director know I've accepted your letter of resignation. Word will get out that you were killed in a drug bust, in which several other members of the Juarez Cartel were also killed. Be good to yourself Brody. I hope you and Officer Rodriguez are happy together."

CHAPTER 30

"Ines."

I was slow to respond to Estelle. My mind was elsewhere. On Brody. I missed him.

"Ines!" I jerked at her sharp tone and looked over at her. "How long are you going to make him suffer?"

I sighed. "I don't know. He kept a huge secret from me, E."

It had been four days since Brody's release from the hospital. I'd made Victor keep me updated. He'd thrown up his hands yesterday and scolded me like I was a recalcitrant child. "I'm done with playing the middle man. Grow a pair and go talk to him. That or let the man down so you can both move on with your lives."

Which was why I was sitting on Estelle's couch, drowning my sorrows in a pint of mint chocolate chip ice cream. I thought maybe she'd be more sympathetic than my brother. Apparently, I thought wrong.

"I get it. I really do. But you have to understand where he was coming from. You're a cop, Ines. You were only undercover for a few weeks. Brody had been a part of the cartel for *years*. He was ingrained in the business. You know the danger you faced just trying to look for Ernesto. A cop they *killed*, and he'd only been investigating them. Brody was a part of Mr. Álvarez's family. Ernie was just looking to make an arrest. Brody was there to bring the entire organization crumbling to the ground. I don't know about you, but I can't even begin to comprehend the stress he had to be under. Especially knowing that he was now in charge of protecting you. To make sure *your* identity wasn't found out."

I swallowed down my bite of ice cream. "I didn't ask him to protect me. I can take care of myself."

Lord, even I cringed at the whine in my voice.

Estelle moved from her spot on the couch and scooted next to me, laying her hand over mine. "Ines, you know I love you."

I set down my ice cream and rested my head on her shoulder. "I know. I love you too. I hate when you're right though. It's not fair you're this smart. What did I ever do to deserve you?"

She laughed. "I promise I'm not that smart. I'm just an objective bystander who can see Brody's side of things. Look at the steps you took to protect me. It had to have been ten times harder for him. Give him a chance. That man loves you. And you love him."

I sighed. "I really do. God, I hate when Victor's right."

That made Estelle snort.

"I need to go see him don't I? Like soon."

She hugged my shoulder. "No time like the present."

I sighed in resignation knowing she was right. "What if he's not home?"

"Then you go back tomorrow. And the next day. Until you guys finally talk."

AN HOUR LATER, I STOOD OUTSIDE BRODY'S HOUSE, MY KNEES practically shaking and a nervous churning in my stomach when I noticed a light on. I thought back to that first night and how everything about it now made sense. Why there was such an unused feel to the house. Because Brody had brought me to *his* house. Not Tomás', but Brody's. I didn't want to read too much into it, but I felt like it meant something. I wiped a sweaty palm on my pants and, with only a minor hesitation, knocked on the door. And waited. And waited some more. Still, the door remained closed without a peep coming from inside. Of course, it was my luck he wasn't home. I moved to leave and only made it down the first step when I heard the lock disengage and the door opened.

"Ines?"

God, just the sound of his voice sent shivers racing through me. I'd missed that voice. I'd missed *him*.

I turned back around and, Sweet Jesus, just about swallowed my tongue. Standing there barefoot, in only a pair of low-slung gray sweatpants, which did nothing to hide, well, *anything*, and his arm in a sling, was Brody.

"Um, hi." I gave a little awkward wave. Fuck, I was turning into a damn girl. Squaring my shoulders, I started again. "Can I come in?"

He stepped back and gestured. "Of course."

I strolled past him and couldn't help but inhale his clean,

masculine scent. Damn, my knees went weak. I wondered if he'd just recently got out of the shower. *Focus, Ines.*

"Can I get you something to drink?" he asked from the doorway to the kitchen.

I shook my head. "No, thanks. Do you mind if I sit?"

"Make yourself at home."

I settled on the couch and glanced around. Seeing the place in the light of day, it appeared different. More lived-in, I guess. Although that was most likely since the tabletops had been dusted and the carpet looked recently vacuumed. There was also the hint of an artificial air freshener mixed with the continued hint of disuse. I'm sure it would take a bit for the smell to dissipate. Brody took the chair opposite from me. Neither one of us spoke, and it was an uncomfortable silence. Something we'd never experienced.

It looked like it was going to be up to me to start the conversation since I'm the one who showed up here. I looked at his bound arm, and all the emotions of a few days ago came rushing back. Worry, fear, anger. It took a moment to get them all under control.

"How are you feeling?" Such an innocuous question, but I figured it was better than the awkward silence.

Brody chuckled softly. "Like I got my ass handed to me."

I couldn't help but smile.

"But seriously, I'm doing okay. I start therapy in a couple weeks for the shoulder, so I'm stuck in this sling until then. I have some aches and pains here and there, but nothing I can't handle." He shrugged. "Otherwise, I'm making it. How about you?"

God, I hated this stilted, polite conversation. Even when he and I were butting heads, we had more spark between us.

Now, it was like we were almost strangers. Inside, my stomach hurt. Especially because I knew that this void was all my fault. I was the jerk who hadn't even come to visit him in the hospital. I was struggling to get past the hurt. I knew Estelle and Victor were right, but it was still painful that Brody hadn't shared a part of himself with me.

I shifted uncomfortably and ignored his question. "I'm sorry I didn't come to the hospital. I should have been there for you."

It was important that he knew that.

"I get it. I'm sure everything came as a shock to you. I'm sorry I didn't tell you I was an undercover agent."

There it was. The giant elephant in the room. Looked like we were going to tackle the subject head on.

"Why?" I tried not to let my hurt feelings show, but I knew I was transparent and Brody could see right through me.

He rubbed a hand down his face in a gesture of fatigue and deep thought, letting out a huff of air and shrugging like he couldn't pinpoint anything specific. "For so many reasons. Shame. Guilt. Fear."

I zeroed in on a single word. "What do you mean, shame?"

He stared at the floor, refusing to meet my eyes. "I was a member of law enforcement. I'd sworn to uphold the law and bring down criminals. When you've been as far under-cover as I've been, you don't just play a role, Ines. You become the role or you die. There are days I woke up hating who I'd become, the things I've done. But, in the end, I ignored it because I didn't want to look too closely at the choices I'd made. I should have resisted the drugs, the killing. Instead, I became immune to them. When I killed Paulo, I should have been horrified by what I'd done. I wasn't. Not then. Not now. In fact, I would do it all over again. Being undercover made me weak. I'm no better than the people I was trying to bring down."

I leapt up from the couch and dropped to my knees in front of Brody, clasping his hand in mine. It finally hit me what Victor and Estelle had been trying to tell me.

"Stop that nonsense this instance. You were in an untenable position. I can't even imagine how you were able to do it all those years. I would have broken a long time ago. You're stronger than you think, Brody."

He finally focused on me, a sad smile on his face, as he reached out to cup my cheek. "The one truly good thing I've done in the last five years was protect you the only way I knew how. Keep the truth from you. You not knowing I was D.E.A. kept you alive."

I covered his hand with mine and leaned into his touch before turning my head to kiss his palm. "I know it was. At first, I was so hurt that you kept it from me. I mean, you knew so much about me, and I barely got to scratch the surface of who you were. And then to hear it from Alejandro, of all people? It just really hurt."

"I'm sorry, baby. I wanted to tell you, but I couldn't bring myself to. I hope you can forgive me."

Instead of giving Brody words, I leaned up and brought my lips to his. Forgiveness was in my very touch. Getting to my feet, I reached for his hand and pulled him to stand. I reached up to kiss him again and then dropped back down to my knees, pulling his sweatpants down with me. I licked my lips in appreciation of the gorgeous sight in front of me.

Not giving him time to do anything, I gripped his shaft in my hand at the same time I leaned forward and ran my tongue up his length, circling the head before engulfing it fully in my mouth.

I worshipped Brody with my lips and tongue, savoring his musky flavor. I traced the vein on the underside of his cock, squeezing the base with exquisite tension. As much as I wanted to suck him dry, I needed him inside me even more.

"Sit." I gently nudged his bare chest at the same time I issued my directive.

Brody followed my command, his legs spread, his good arm resting along the back of the couch. He looked entirely too comfortable. I wanted him as desperate for me as I was for him. Slowly, I gave a little strip tease, giving him tantalizing glimpses of bare skin before covering it up again and teasing him with a new location of skin. Soon, his eyes were feverish with need and he was breathing hard. It was time to stop teasing us both. I gripped my shirt and ripped it up and over my head, my unbound breasts fully in view. Then, came my pants and underwear. I kicked off my shoes before stepping out of the circle of clothes at my feet.

I moved in and straddled his lap, rocking myself against him. Brody cursed at the sensation.

"I don't have a condom."

I stopped moving for a moment. "I'm on the pill, and I haven't been with anyone else in a while."

"You're the only woman I've slept with in five years."

At that pronouncement, my mouth fell open. "What? Are you serious? I mean, not that there's anything wrong with that. I'm just…surprised."

Brody shrugged, a tinge of a blush still gracing his cheeks. "I've been kind of busy is all."

I cupped his cheeks and stared into his eyes. "I'm glad. Now, I want you to touch me."

His expression shifted and a devious smile appeared. He moved his free hand off the back of the couch and placed it on my thigh, squeezing gently before skimming it up and down my body, wherever he could reach. Everywhere but where I wanted him to touch me most. My core throbbed, and I begged against his lips.

"Please."

His mouth broke from mine, but his fingers continued their path up my thigh, stopping just short of where I was desperate for his touch.

"Please, what?"

I groaned in torturous agony when his finger ghosted across my clit. I arched into the touch, needing more contact, but Brody pulled back.

"Touch me, damn it." I thrust my pelvis forward, my fingernails digging into his bicep.

This time, his hand reached out to cup my breast, his thumb flicking my nipple, shooting a spark of pleasure through me.

"Here?"

"No, you jerk, here." My hand found its way to my core, the place I wanted him the most, and I shoved two fingers inside me, needing to feel my pussy clenching on something.

"Fuck me, that's hot." His voice was gravelly with arousal. "But isn't that my job?"

I threw my head back when I gave another thrust of my

digits. "I was tired of waiting on you."

He chuckled at my sassy remark. "Well, wait no longer."

A moan erupted from deep inside me when one of his fingers joined mine.

"Oh god," I cried out when a second one joined the other three. My pussy had never felt so full as it did with four fingers pushing deep inside me. I clenched my muscles, trying to keep him inside me when he made to pull them out. I was stretched so wide, and the ache that started in my belly spread. When Brody's thumb rubbed circles around my clit, I was lost. I screamed when the orgasm hit. Rainbow colored lights burst behind my eyes and my pussy spasmed with the force of my climax.

"You're so beautiful. You know that, right?"

"You make me feel beautiful." I gasped when he pulled out his fingers. I followed suit. "I need you inside me. I need you to fuck me. Now."

Without waiting for a response, I lowered myself onto his engorged cock. He rocked upwards a few times, too slowly for my liking, torturing me in the process. Having none of it, I raised up on my knees before slamming myself back down onto him. I cried out his name in ecstasy when he entered me entirely.

Once again, I clenched my muscles, this time causing him to moan low.

"Now, fuck me."

Brody raised a single eyebrow and gave me a cocky, satisfied smile. "Yes, ma'am."

He gripped my hip, hard, and began to thrust upward. His mouth met mine again, his tongue darting inside to match the rhythm of his cock pounding into my pussy. He continued his assault on my body as he reached between us to circle my clit. Tension built when he hit that right spot deep inside. I met his thrusts with downward ones of my own and as the pressure spread through me and another orgasm rushed through me like a volcanic eruption. Brody thrust a few more times and then his climax hit. His seed washed my insides and small tremors continued to rock my body as his movements slowed and became less deep.

I collapsed against his sweat-covered chest, our breathing ragged. We both groaned when I shifted and his cock jerked inside me. I pulled back and dismounted, but he refused to let me go far, so I sat on his lap, his arms wrapped around me. I laid my head on his shoulder and basked in the feeling of closeness.

"I resigned from the agency."

I lifted my head. "Why?"

"It just didn't feel right to be a part of it anymore. I'm not the same man I was when I joined. It's not something I think I could do anymore. Not now."

I laid my hand on Brody's chest, tracing the spot where his heart was. "What do you want to do?"

He inhaled and let it all out. "I was thinking Colorado sounded like a beautiful place."

My fingers stopped moving. "Really? What about us?"

He brushed my sweat-dampened hair off my face, his eyes searching my face. "I know it's a lot to ask, but I was kind of hoping you'd come with me. You don't have to give me an answer today. I know it's a lot to take in. I just want you to think about it."

"Yes."

Now it was his turn to appear surprised. "Are…are you sure?"

I feverishly nodded my head, smiling brightly. "Definitely. I'll go wherever you are, Brody. I love you."

It struck me then, I'd never told him that. Of course, neither had he, but this felt right. He laughed and kissed me like crazy.

"God, Ines, I love you so much. You've made me so happy. I have no idea what I'm going to do there, but I know I'll figure something out. I have a comfortable savings, so we'll be okay for a while."

I laughed right along with him. "*We'll* figure something out. We're a team now Brody, you and me. You're not alone anymore."

CHAPTER 31

I'd received a phone call from Preston a few days ago telling me he was leaving Pleasant Village. He'd reached the point in his recovery where he felt ready for the real world again. This was his second time leaving the Village, and I prayed it was the last. That he could find a reason to stay clean. To date, his longest sober streak was four years. I'd respected his wishes to not come visit again, but during our talk I'd asked him if I could please visit before he left. I'd told him there was someone I wanted to introduce to him. I'd actually been surprised he'd agreed to us coming.

"Are you nervous?"

Ines squeezed my hand as we stood outside the familiar white building I hadn't seen in months.

"A little. We didn't part on the best of terms the last time I was here. I'm in a different place than I was then. I just...I just don't want to fuck things up."

"Hey, I'm here if things get tense. Everything is going to be fine."

Her words helped me steel my spine, and I kissed our

joined hands, thankful for this woman in my life. "I love you."

She smiled brilliantly at me before half-leading me into the building. The echo of our footsteps sounded throughout the foyer until we were finally at the front desk, where the ever-helpful Mary sat. She smiled when she looked up from her desk, but it faltered when she saw the shape I was in. The bruises on my face were fading, but still obvious, and my arm was supported in an immobilizer. She quickly recovered, especially when her gaze landed on Ines.

"Welcome back, Mr. Thomas. We've missed you these last couple months. And who is this lovely lady?"

"Hi, Mary. This is Ines."

"It's a pleasure to meet you, Mary."

"You as well. Preston will be so happy to see the two of you. He's out in the garden. Would you like an escort?"

I shook my head, smiling to soften the denial. "No, thank you. I know the way."

The smell of honeysuckle wafted through the air as we weaved our way along the path toward the center. We turned a corner and there he was. Looking the same, yet different. Stronger. Preston looked over at our approach and love for my brother rushed through me. I waited for the bitterness to follow, but oddly, it remained at bay. His eyes darted between me and my condition and Ines, and I could see the question in them. I hadn't told him who I was bringing, only that I wanted him to meet someone.

When we came abreast of him, my tongue suddenly stuck to the roof of my mouth and I had trouble speaking. Luckily, Ines took control. She reached out her hand, greeting Preston like an old friend.

"Hi, I'm Ines. I'm so glad to finally meet you. Your brother has told me all about you."

I finally found my voice. "It's really good to see you."

And for the first time since our mother's death, I pulled my brother into a hug, holding on tightly, completely disregarding the stinging discomfort in my shoulder. I don't even know how long we stood there embracing, but a sniffle from Ines reminded me where we were. Reluctantly, I pulled back not even realizing until that moment that my eyes were damp. A quick glance confirmed the same for Preston. We both self-consciously cleared our throats.

"Would you like to have a seat?"

Ines sat on the end, pulling me down next to her so I sat sandwiched between her and my brother when he took his place. Once we were seated, she continued holding my hand like she was lending me her strength.

"Thank you for letting me come visit. I know things have been…tense between us for a long time. I haven't been a very good brother. There's been so much unnecessary blame, which is my fault. I've had a lot of bitterness building inside me. For that, I'm sorry."

Preston sat back against the wooden bench, a dazed expression on his face. "Wow, this is a little bit of a surprise. I'm not sure what to say."

"You don't have to say anything. I just hope you can forgive me. For everything. Maybe not today. But someday. I want us to be brothers again."

He sat silently, absorbing my words. There were so many things I wanted to share with him. About my life over the last ten years. About Ines. I also wanted to get to know him better.

"I think I'd like that." Until Preston actually said the words, I didn't realize how much I wanted this. I released Ines' hand and pulled him in for another hug. It felt really good.

"So, what are your plans for when you leave here?"

His shrug was non-committal. "Honestly, I have no idea. I mean, I don't have a lot of life skills, you know? I talked to my sponsor, and she has some construction work lined up for me, but that's not something I want to do forever. It will get me by for a while and pay the bills, so I'm not going to complain."

"Where will you be staying?"

"There's a halfway house that has an open bed for practically nothing. I just have to help keep the place up along with certain chores. It's part of the deal to live there."

"Ines and I are leaving Chicago and heading to Colorado. You could always come with us. We could all start over."

I wasn't sure who was more surprised by the offer, Preston or me. Well, maybe Ines, considering the offer just popped out. It wasn't something she and I had discussed prior to coming here, but I knew how important family was to her, and I was sure she wouldn't balk at the idea. She confirmed my thought when she spoke over my shoulder.

"We'd love to have you. I know Brody would really like to get to know you better. As would I."

Preston continued to appear slightly off balance. I had a feeling our expressions matched.

"Wow. This is such a surprise. Let me think on it. I don't want to impose."

"It wouldn't be an imposition at all. But I understand

needing to think about it. It's an important decision, and you have to do what's right for you. Whatever decision you make, please know I'm here for you."

He nodded. "I appreciate that. So, why don't you tell me how you two met."

Ines and I stayed a little while longer to chat, giving Preston the abridged version of our meeting. We didn't go into detail, figuring it was best left for another time. When it was time for us to leave, we promised to get together again before we left for Colorado if he chose not to come with us. While Ines and I walked out to the car, I truly felt, for the first time in years, that Preston and I were going to be okay, and that I finally had my brother back.

CHAPTER 32

It had been two weeks since Alejandro's death and Miguel's escape. There was a nationwide APB out on him, but he'd gone deep underground. Who knew how long it would take him to emerge and start to rebuild, because we both knew he would. He craved money and power too much not to.

In the meantime, life was moving forward. For obvious reasons, I stopped working at *Sweet SINoritas.* But I hated that I'd left Michele in the dark about why I was no longer there and who I really was. I'd grown to care for her over the last few months, and the guilt ate at me that the last time I'd seen her was when I was being loaded into an ambulance. She had no idea what had happened to me. Which was why I was standing in the doorway of the ladies' locker room.

"Hey."

Michele looked up in surprise at my soft-spoken greeting. She rushed over, robe swinging behind her like a cape, and threw her arms around me. "Oh my god, Gabby! I've been so worried about you. Damon told me you were taking some time off after Alejandro's attack, but it's been forever and I hadn't heard from you. I had no idea if you'd be back or not. And I had no idea how to get a hold of you. You never gave me your phone number. How come you never gave me your phone number? I needed to make sure—"

"Michele, stop," I interrupted her babbling, although my arms had returned her embrace. Her continued rambling only made the guilt run deeper.

She complied with my request and pulled back, looking at the newly formed scar on my face. I'd had the stitches removed last week, and it was still a little tender. I also still had a yellowish bruise along my jawline. Her expression changed to one of anger. "I hate him for what he did to you. I don't understand why he did this."

I wondered how much I should tell her. Next to Estelle, she was one of my closest friends. I just hoped she didn't hate me after I told her the truth. Praying I wasn't going to regret this, I took her hand.

"Let's go outside and talk."

She continued to wear a worried expression, but she followed my lead through the doors until we stood in the parking lot. Despite it being May, the air was still chilly in the evenings, especially with the breeze coming in off the lake. I cursed at myself, forgetting how little Michele wore. She was probably freezing.

"On second thought, maybe we should go inside. You have to be cold." I started to tug her back toward inside, but she waved me off.

"I'm fine. Just tell me what's going on, Gabby. You're scaring me."

"I want you to know that I never meant to hurt you in any way." I inhaled, not knowing where to start. I guess with the easiest thing. "My name isn't Gabriela."

Michele drew back in confusion. "What are you talking about?"

"My real name is Ines Rodriguez. I'm an officer with the Chicago PD, and I've been undercover for the last few months while I searched for my brother."

Confusion cleared replaced with first, shock and then the sharpest emotion of all. Hurt.

"You mean—" Michele's voice cracked and then rose with accusation "—you lied to me? All this time you've been lying to me?"

I tried to clasp her hands, but she pulled them back, clutching them into fists at her side as though holding in her pain. Her breath came in short bursts.

"I didn't want to, I swear."

Her eyes glistened with tears as she raged. "You know how I feel about liars and you did it anyway."

She was right. I knew how she felt. Not why, but I definitely knew how she felt, especially after that night at the el. My shoulders sagged in defeat.

"I'm sorry. I was desperate to find Ernesto. He was my main priority. Then, I got to know you and you became my friend. But, Michele, you have to understand. I was doing *my job*. It wasn't meant to hurt you. I was protecting myself and trying to protect my brother. Do you know what Alejandro would have done to me if he knew I was a cop? They'd already killed Ernesto. He would have killed me, too. Or worse. If I'd told you who I really was, you might be dead. Maybe even Maisy. You have to understand. Everything I've done is to protect the people I care about. Including you."

My eyes begged for a forgiveness I prayed was granted. I tried again to reach out for her, holding my breath and praying. I almost cried when she let me wrap my hands around hers. Then, without warning, she threw her arms around me. I did the same and we were both sobbing against the other's shoulder. When our tears dried, she pulled away and wiped a stray drop from her lashes.

"I understand why you did what you had to do. It still hurts, but I understand. What happens now? Are you safe? Did Alejandro find out about you? Oh my god, are you in danger coming here?"

"I'm safe. Alejandro can't hurt anyone ever again. He's burning in hell where he belongs. Do you remember the night this happened?" I gestured to my face.

She turned another grief-stricken glance at my scar. "How could I forget? That was the scariest night of my life."

"Mine too. But for more reasons than just a cut on my face. He threatened someone I'd come to care for. Someone else who was keeping secrets."

I let her puzzle it out. Her eyes widened and she breathed out his name. "Tomás."

I nodded. "That's part of the reason I was gone for so long. Alejandro was holding him captive. Torturing him. Because of his secrets."

"Tomás wasn't who he said he was, was he?"

Michele never ceased to amaze me with how smart she was. "Who is he?"

"His name is Brody Thomas. He's D.E.A. Was, anyway."

She looked gobsmacked. I didn't blame her. I was still a

little shell-shocked over everything that had happened over the last week, and I was there for it. I should be used to the news of who Brody really was, but there were moments I was still wrapping my head around it.

"So, what happens now?"

"Well, I hope we can remain friends." I was almost shy in my request.

Michele smiled and my heart grew lighter. "I'd really like that."

"Me too." I reached out and squeezed her hand. "There was another reason I came by tonight. I wanted to let you know that Brody and I are leaving town. We're going to settle somewhere new. Somewhere safe."

Michele's face dropped. "When are you leaving?"

I smiled sadly back at her. "In the morning."

She threw her arms around me, hugging me tightly. "I'm going to miss you."

"I'll miss you too. But if there is ever anything you need, please know you can call me."

Michele and I exchanged phone numbers and I left her with the promise I'd call her soon. Once she'd gone back inside, I turned to where my love waited for me. I slipped on my leather jacket and helmet before climbing on the back of the Softail.

"I'm glad you were able to see her before we left." Brody squeezed the hands I'd wrapped around his waist. He'd finally stopped wearing his sling.

"Me too." Sadness crept in behind the exhilaration of beginning a new life. I hugged Brody tighter as he cranked up the bike, its engine roaring loud in the otherwise quiet parking lot. "I'm both sad and excited about going home to

Colorado though. Chicago is such a great city, but I miss the mountains and wide open spaces."

He pulled out and headed toward my dad's house. We planned on spending our last night in town with my family.

"We can come back and visit. It's best that we get out of town for a while. At least until Miguel is caught."

"I know. I just hope it's soon."

EPILOGUE

Six months later

The sky was a fiery burst of reds, oranges, and yellows as the sun set behind the mountainous horizon. I reclined against the warm body behind me, Brody's arms wrapped tightly around my waist, while we sat on our wraparound porch absorbing the beauty in front of us. The last few months had been full of peace and tranquility, something we'd both earned, especially Brody. He was still struggling with the guilt of some of the things he'd done while undercover, but slowly he was learning to forgive himself. He also was trying hide his disappointment that Preston had chosen to go back home to Chicago, even though they spoke a couple times a week. The ringing phone interrupted our solace.

I swiped right and greeted my brother. "Hey Victor."

"Ines."

I jerked upright at his tone. Brody tensed behind me. "What's wrong?"

"Someone tried to kidnap Estelle tonight." He paused, and I knew there was more. "I think it was Miguel."

"Son of a bitch. We're coming home." I'd already risen and hustled into the house to start packing.

"No," he commanded. "Stay where you are. I'm watching over her. If it's Miguel, we'll get him. It's not safe for you right now, especially Brody."

I growled, because I knew he was right, although I wasn't happy about it. "You better keep me updated, and if things get too much, I'm coming back regardless."

"I'll be in touch. I just wanted you to know so you two could keep an eye out, just in case his people find you. Look, we can't talk long. I'll call you soon. Love you."

"Love—" Victor hung up before I could finish.

I wanted to throw the phone across the room, but I settled for slamming it on the couch. I started to pace when Brody pulled me into his arms. I cuddled closer and breathed in his scent, trying to find my control.

"Talk to me, baby." His voice vibrated through his chest against my cheek.

"Estelle may be in danger, and it's all my fault. Victor thinks it was Miguel, and there's nothing I can do about it right now. He thinks we need to stay here, and I'm pissed because he's right. If we step back into Chicago and Miguel *is* there, you're a dead man, and most likely me right along with you."

I softened in Brody's embrace, especially when he stroked my hair and kissed the top of my head. "She has Victor. You know he'll protect her with his life."

"I know, but it still hurts that I can't be there to help." I sniffled a tear back.

"She'll be okay. You have to believe that."

"I'm just scared."

Brody pulled back and cupped my cheeks in his strong hands, wiping away a stray tear with his thumb. "The best thing you can do for Estelle is to be safe. She wouldn't want you to sacrifice yourself for her. Trust Victor."

"I do. He's in love with her. I know he'll do everything he can to make sure she stays safe."

"Just continue to remind yourself that, and everything will be okay." He leaned down to ghost a kiss across my lips. "C'mon, let's go check on the herd and then we'll head to bed. Things will look better in the morning. I promise."

I stared up at this man I loved more than anything. "How did I get so lucky to find you?"

His smile lit up his face. "I ask myself that every day. Except I'm the lucky one. I love you Ines Maite Rodriguez."

"I love you too."

I temporarily pushed away all thoughts of danger and walked hand in hand outside to check on our stock. Never in a million years did I imagine I'd give up being a police officer to raise cattle in the wilds of Colorado with the man I loved. The lowing sounds made by our cows was a vast change from the city sounds of a bustling Chicago.

But I'd found more happiness out here than I ever thought possible. Here, with Brody, was where I belonged.

Thank you so much for reading IN TOO DEEP! I hope you

enjoyed it. If so, I'd greatly appreciate a review on the platform of your choice. Reviews are so important!

Now that Estelle's in danger, Victor is watching over her. But what happens when two people who are fighting their love for one another remain in close quarters for too long?

You can find out in STRIKING DISTANCE
Book 2 in the Love Undercover series
https://amzn.to/2Ct8f1h

Turn the page for a preview.

STRIKING DISTANCE

FAINT SHADOWS WERE CAST across the pavement as I hoofed it across the nearly deserted parking lot, tugging my messenger bag full of graded papers against my hip. The closer I got to my car, the faster my steps grew, and a trickle of uneasiness settled over me. The air thickened with a heavy tension that threatened to choke me. Even the normally chirping critters who came out at dusk were quiet and still. I scanned my surroundings, but there were only a few cars scattered here and there.

Cursing myself for overreacting, I slowed my steps and ignored the lead weight in my belly. I reached my car and tossed my bag across the inside of the vehicle to land with a thud on the passenger seat.

A warm, strong hand clapped over my mouth. My scream was muffled behind the tight grip. I scratched and clawed at the other hand that wrapped around my waist pulling me away from the safety of my car. The strong scent of expensive cologne hit my nose, and heavily accented words pierced my eardrums despite my struggles and strangled cries for help. "You may not be that *puta*, but you'll lead me to her."

My heels dragged along the pavement. My chest burned with the need to pull in air. My brain screamed at me to think. A surge of adrenaline kicked in, and I called on all the self-defense techniques Ines had taught me. I fought back, slamming my head backward as hard as I could. The crunch of my skull connecting with the face behind me sounded loud in my ears, but I didn't have time to savor it.

"Mierda!" The curse came out nasally.

My body went totally limp, and I slid out of his grip, dropping to my knees. I quickly rammed my elbow up and into the groin of my assailant. Ignoring his bellow of pain, I jumped to my feet and ran as fast as I could back to the school, my ragged breaths echoing through the cool evening air.

I raced down the hallways, hollering. "Somebody, help!"

I collided with a soft body, and my scream was piercing.

"Ms. Jenkins, what's wrong?"

I pulled back at Willie's voice. "Call 9-1-1 now. Someone just tried to grab me in the parking lot."

"Shit. Come on." He tugged me into the nearby janitor closet and locked the door behind us. I wrapped my arms around myself to try and control my shivering while he pulled a cell phone out of his pocket. "Are you okay?"

I absently nodded, my entire focus on the door, and prayed the unknown man didn't try and enter. I only vaguely heard Willie talking next to me.

"The police are on their way."

I blinked and locked eyes with him still holding the phone to his ear. At his words, my adrenaline high crashed, and I burst into tears. He wrapped an arm around me, and I cried against his shoulder. My tears eventually stopped. Pounding footsteps and loud voices interrupted the silence. "Secure the area. Check every nearby room."

We waited. Finally we heard a chorus of "All clear."

A loud knock on the door made me jump.

"Police, is everyone all right?"

Willie opened the door, keeping me behind him. I spotted the first uniformed officer over his shoulder, and my body sagged in relief. My eyes moved to the second man, and my heart skipped a beat, then started another wild pulsing in my chest. *Victor.*

The first officer shifted, blocking my view, and our connection was severed. "Miss? Is everyone okay?"

"Yes," I focused on his words. "Sorry."

"I'm Officer Gladstone and this is my partner, Officer Rodriguez. Can you tell me your name?"

"Estelle Jenkins."

"Miss Jenkins, why don't we step in here and you can tell us what happened?"

He gestured to the nearest classroom and pulled out a notepad.

"Do you need me for anything?" Willie asked.

The two officers exchanged glances and Gladstone shook his head. "Not at the moment, but we may call you in to answer some questions."

"I'll be here a little while longer. Come find me. I'm glad you're okay Ms. Jenkins."

"Thank you for your help, Willie." I hugged him before he disappeared down the hall.

I led us inside while Gladstone called into dispatch, acutely aware of Victor on my heels.

"Our forensics team is on the way. Now, I understand someone grabbed you in the parking lot. Can you tell me anything about your assailant? Man or woman? Height? Hair color? Any details you can recall would be extremely helpful, no matter how small you think it might be."

"It all happened so fast. Definitely a man. He came up from behind me, so I didn't get a look at him. Once I got free, I just ran."

"Do you mind if I ask how you escaped?" He paused in his writing.

"I dropped to my knees and shoved my elbow straight into his nuts. Then I took off running."

Both men winced and shifted uncomfortably.

"Oh, there is one thing. He spoke with a heavy Spanish accent. Called me a *puta*. Said something about me not being her, but I can't recall his exact words. I'm sorry."

Finally, Victor spoke. "It could have been Miguel Álvarez."

I sucked in a breath. My gaze darted to meet his. "After all this time? Why now? And how would he even know about me? I never met him personally. Only Alejandro, and he's dead."

Victor scoffed. "The D.E.A. has been looking for Álvarez since he escaped, but rumor has it he's been spending these last months doing everything he can to rebuild his empire. He still has loyal employees. Ones who no doubt saw you with Ines. She never should have stayed in contact with you while she was undercover. He knows he can use you to get to her."

He paced, running one hand through his hair, and it was then I finally noticed how tense he was. His jaw was clenched, and I'd never seen that expression on his face before. It was filled with so much rage. His brown eyes were as dark as pitch, and his fists were balled at his sides.

A throat cleared and we both glanced over at the other officer I'd forgotten was in the room. His gaze darted between the two of us. "Does someone want to fill me in on what you two are talking about? It's obvious you know each other, and have intel I don't."

"It's possible our perp is Miguel Álvarez."

Gladstone's eyes bulged. "As in the head of the Juárez Cartel? Why the fuck would he want to kidnap Miss Jenkins?" He darted an abashed glance in my direction. "Pardon the language, ma'am."

I waved him off. It wasn't like I hadn't heard the word before. I was practically raised in the Rodriguez household. One made entirely of boys, aside from Ines.

Victor gave his partner a brief rundown. "It was kept quiet, but about eight months ago, my sister went undercover to find our missing brother. When it was all said and done, Álvarez escaped, and his nephew, Alejandro, was dead. His entire empire was taken down by an undercover D.E.A. agent. My guess is he wants revenge against my sister and Brody. Estelle is the key to that."

"No way. I'm not the key to anything. I don't know anything of value to him. I don't even know exactly where Ines and Brody are. They said it was safer that way."

"It's possible Álvarez thinks otherwise."

The door opened. Both men went for their weapons at the same time. Victor pulled me behind him. A man wearing a forensics shirt stepped into the room, and everyone relaxed. Guns were put away.

"We're still processing the scene, but we found this on the ground outside the vehicle." He held out my messenger bag. "We didn't bother dusting it for fingerprints due to the fabric. You might want to check and make sure everything's there."

Victor took the bag from his hand and gave it to me. I was careful not to touch him.

"My cell phone and wallet are gone."

He cursed. "He has your ID. He knows where you live."

My stomach sank. "What does that mean?"

Officer Gladstone answered. "It means you go home and hope this was a random incident."

"And if it wasn't?"

He put his notepad back in his pocket. "If you're uncomfortable with that idea, we can request a patrol car to periodically stop by and check on you. A more drastic option, and more difficult one to get approved, is you can request to stay in a safe house."

"Or you can stay with us," Victor added.

My eyes darted over to meet his, and I was already shaking my head. No way was I staying at the Rodriguez house. Not with Victor there. I'd take my chances requesting either a patrol car or a safe house.

I turned to Gladstone. "If a safe house was approved, what all would that entail?"

Get your copy of STRIKING DISTANCE today!

https://amzn.to/2Ct8f1h

Doms of Club Eden

Submission

Desire

Redemption

Protect

Betrayal

My Christmas Dom

Absolution

Forever (A prequel) - Coming July 2020

Love Undercover Series

In Too Deep

Striking Distance

Atonement

Other Books

Love Notes: A Dark Romance

SEALs in Love

Say Yes

Black Light: Possession

Saving Evie: A Brotherhood Protectors

ABOUT THE AUTHOR

LK Shaw resides in South Carolina with her high mainte-
nance beagle mix dog, Miss P. An avid reader since childhood, she became hooked on historical romance novels in
high school. She now reads, and loves, all romance sub-
genres, with dark romance and romantic suspense being
her favorite. LK enjoys traveling and chocolate. Her books
feature hot alpha heroes and the strong women they love.

Want a FREE short story? Be sure to sign up for my newsletter and download your copy of A Birthday Spanking, a
Doms of Club Eden prequel!
http://bit.ly/LKShawNewsletter

LK loves to interact with readers. You can follow her on any
of her social media:

LK Shaw's Club Eden: https://www.facebook.com/
groups/LKShawsClubEden
Author Page: www.facebook.com/LKShawAuthor

Author Profile: www.facebook.com/AuthorLKShaw
IG: @LKShaw_Author
Amazon: www.amazon.com/author/lkshaw
Bookbub: https://www.bookbub.com/authors/lk-shaw
Website: www.lkshawauthor.com

Made in the USA
Columbia, SC
17 June 2020